THE RAT KILLER AND OTHER WEIRD WAR TALES
By Sean McLachlan

For Almudena and Julián, as always

INTRODUCTION

The battlefield is a strange place, a place of overpowering sensations and unreal sights. Men and women in combat know death is close and it becomes easy to believe in the supernatural. And it's not just the combatants who are affected. Those left behind on the home front often resort to arcane rituals to contact loved ones they have lost.

During the American Civil War, there was a great surge in the use of mediums and séances, something I have written about in an article for *Black Gate* magazine titled "Spiritualism during the American Civil War[1]". Every home and battleground seemed to have had its ghost, and many remain haunted to this day.

While science can't explain these talks with the dead, and rarely bothers to try, some supernatural events have been explained by thorough research. After the bloody Battle of Shiloh on 6-7 April 1862, there were such terrible casualties that hundreds of men were left out in the swampy fields overnight. Some weren't found for several nights and lay in agony, soaked by a downpour and chilled by the cool spring air.

As they lay there, wondering if they would live to see their homes again, many saw something strange. At night their wounds began to glow with a faint greenish-blue light. The overstretched medical personnel in both armies noticed this too. They also noticed that those men whose wounds glowed had a better survival rate, recovered more quickly, and scarred less than those men whose wounds didn't glow. The strange phosphorescence was dubbed a miracle and called "Angel's Glow."

The story was tucked away into the dusty back shelf of historical memory, considered a miracle by those who believe in such things and a folktale by everyone else. That is, until two high school students named William Martin and Jonathan Curtis decided to dedicate their Science Fair project to the mystery. Martin's mother was a microbiologist and

---

1.   https://www.blackgate.com/2012/09/19/spiritualism-during-the-american-civil-war/

helped point the way, but the kids did most of the work and certainly deserve most of the credit.

They knew that soil is filled with microscopic worms called nematodes. These worms like to burrow into insects and vomit a certain bacteria called *Photorhabdus luminescens*, which acts as a poison against the insect and other types of bacteria. When the insect dies, the nematodes have a feast. Isn't nature lovely? Interestingly, *Photorhabdus luminescens* glows in the dark.

So Martin and Curtis theorized that insects were attracted to the open wound, a common occurrence on the battlefield, and the nematodes in turn attacked the insects, spilling their vomitus, glowing bacteria into the wounds. This sanitized the wounds and helped the men recover. *Photorhabdus luminescens* can't survive in warm temperatures, which is why we don't see glowing wounds more often, but the casualties at Shiloh had been exposed to cold conditions for hours or even days and many probably suffered from hypothermia. Those men whose wounds didn't glow had either been collected earlier or had somehow kept sheltered from the rain and cold. While this might have made them more comfortable, they didn't enjoy the advantage of worms throwing up in their wounds!

Other supernatural war stories have less scientific, more unusual explanations. During the World War One Battle of Mons on 22–23 August 1914, the British Expeditionary force first pushed back and then was outflanked by the German Army. The British were soon in full retreat and barely managed to escape without being destroyed. Several months after the battle, when the war had already degenerated into trench warfare, a rumor spread that the retreating British had seen ghostly archers shooting at the Germans and helping the British troops get away. There were even tales of Germans being found with arrows stuck into their bodies. Were these the angels of British longbowmen from Crécy and Agincourt, fighting for England once more?

Actually, the truth is more mundane but no less odd. On 29 September 1914, the writer Arthur Machen, famous for his weird tales, published a short story called "The Bowmen" in the newspaper *The Evening News.* The story was written as a first-person account of an unnamed soldier calling on St. George to save his army, at which point the ghosts of Agincourt appear and start firing volleys at the Germans. The story was not labeled as fiction and Machen had written many nonfiction articles about the war, so it took on the air of a false documentary, a bit like *The Blair Witch Project.*

The idea of angelic warriors saving the British army caught the popular imagination. Machen's story was reprinted countless times, and the story grew with every telling. Soon other people were adding their "eyewitness" accounts to the affair, and while Machen did his best to tell everyone he had made the story up, no one was listening anymore. The story had gotten away from him.

In retrospect, it's not really that surprising. By early 1915, when the story became popular, most people on the home front had realized there would be no quick victory over the Germans. The boys had not come home for Christmas and in all likelihood would not come home next Christmas either. As casualties mounted, people needed to be reassured that God was on their side. The legend of the Bowmen of Mons gave them that faith. It was small comfort for a nation that would lose close to a million men in the Great War.

Three of the stories you'll find in this book are set in that terrible conflict. All involve the Oxford and Buckinghamshire Light Infantry, a regiment that's the focus of my *Trench Raiders*[2] series of novels. Readers of that series will recognize some familiar faces.

The first and longest story is "The Rat Killer", which while it skirts into the territory of the paranormal is based on a sad reality. The rats that plagued the trenches on the Western Front got so bad that

---

2.   *https://www.amazon.com/gp/product/B07FRTSFT9*

regiments actually did have fulltime rat killers tasked with hunting them down.

The next story, "Call of Nature", follows an odd adventure of Private Howard Black. Readers of the *Trench Raiders* series know him as a tough soldier with a knack for tinkering with machinery and getting his friends out of tight spots. They'll see a new side to him in this story.

The third story, "Sinking", is a short tale about an all-too-common occurrence on the Western Front.

For the next two stories we go back to the nineteenth century. In fact, both happen in 1864, something I didn't actually plan. "Dannevirke" tells the tale of a poorly trained Danish militia defending an old Viking rampart against the far superior Prussian invading force, something that really did occur in the Dano-Prussian War. How they try to tip the scales in their favor is something that hopefully can't happen in the real world.

The final story, "After the Raid", is tied to my Civil War horror novel *A Fine Likeness*[3], although you don't have to read that book to understand or enjoy the story. It recounts an important scene of the novel from a different point of view, focusing on a character who, while pivotal, is only in the novel briefly. It looks at the consequences of our actions and how they can ripple out in unexpected ways.

"Dannevirke" was originally published as a standalone story by Damnation Books under my old pen name Sean J. Lachlan. It is now out of print. "After the Raid" first appeared in the anthology *Spirits of St. Louis: Missouri Ghost Stories*[4]. The three other stories in this book are all appearing for the first time.

Enjoy!

---

3.   *https://www.amazon.com/Fine-Likeness-House-Divided-Book-ebook/dp/B006ANR3TM/*

4.   *https://www.amazon.com/Spirits-St-Louis-Missouri-Stories-ebook/dp/B00GA8W9H8/*

THE RAT KILLER

Sergeant Adam Hook was the best rat killer in the regiment.

He'd killed thousands, maybe tens of thousands. Whenever the Germans weren't attacking, he was on the hunt. It had become his obsession, his crusade. His stretch of trench had the lowest rat population on all the Western Front. Commanders from other regiments bribed his own commander with cigars and bottles of vintage French wine to transfer him to their part of the line for a week or two.

Of course he'd get handsomely paid in the deal too, but he didn't care so much about that. A new bit of trench always offered a challenge.

Take this regiment he was helping now, for example. The Oxfordshire and Buckinghamshire Light Infantry was a fine outfit. They'd given the Hun a bloody nose at Mons and again at the Aisne, and held the line at Ypres when the British Empire was a whisker away from losing the war. Everyone looked up to the Oxs and Bucks.

But they were useless when it came to hunting rats. Disease had become rife in their regiment and finally the commander of their Company E, a Major Thompson, had appealed for help.

Their bit of the line was pretty typical—a muddy network of front line trenches, support trenches a few hundred yards behind those, and communication trenches connecting them. The ground had seen two British offensives and a major German counteroffensive in the past month, plus regular pummeling from German artillery. Corpses littered every muddy pool and blast crater. The reek of decaying flesh hung in the damp French air. Prime breeding ground for rats.

And they were everywhere, scrabbling up the trench walls, nosing into dugouts, bursting from beneath sandbags and equipment whenever someone picked something up. A peek over the parapet with a periscope revealed that the land over the top was teeming with them. Every corpse, every bit of flesh torn off by an artillery shell, made a feast for the little bastards. They liked the trench too, finding shelter from the incessant rain while feasting on the fresh food left carelessly by these men who spent most of their attention worrying about the Germans.

Let them worry about the Germans. Worrying about the rats was his problem.

When he first reported to Major Thompson at the Oxs and Bucks, received his bunk in a reasonably dry dugout, and was slipped a thick envelope that he was too polite to open in Thompson's presence, he made an announcement.

"Sir, I haven't been in your trenches more than ten minutes and I can see you have a serious problem. You know my reputation and you know I can help. You said in your note that you were at my disposal. That's very kind, and very wise."

Major Thompson's face darkened. The upper classes didn't like to be spoken to in this manner by a clerk's son, but Thompson seemed smart enough to know when he needed help. Thompson proved this by keeping his mouth shut and letting Hook continue.

"It's 1700 hours now. Too late to get started in earnest. Tomorrow after breakfast please announce a contest. From the time of the announcement until sunset, all men not on essential duties will devise their own ways to hunt rats. The man who kills the most will win a week off all fatigue duty."

"Sounds like a brilliant idea," Thompson said. "And what will you do?"

"I will observe your men and gauge their strengths and weaknesses. Then in the evening I will show them what they are doing right, and what they are doing wrong. Tonight I have another job to do."

"What's that?"

"Clean out this dugout."

Thompson looked around, confused. The small room with its makeshift bunks for six men, lit by a single candle set atop a table made of packing crates, looked relatively tidy by current standards.

"But I sent two men down here just before you came," Thompson objected. "They must have killed a dozen rats."

"Which have been replaced by two dozen more," Hook said.

In a flash of motion, Hook whipped out his bayonet, stamped his foot on the floor, fell to his knees and jabbed the weapon under the nearest bunk. There was a pitiful squeal. Hook withdrew the bayonet and held it up. Two rats writhed on the blade.

Thompson looked equal parts amazed and disgusted. The balance tipped in favor of disgusted as blood dribbled down the blade to coat Hook's hand.

"How...how did you know where to aim?" Thompson stammered. "You stabbed them without even seeing them!"

Hook looked him in the eye.

"Instinct."

Actually it was simple observation. In his peripheral vision he'd seen the rat's eyes shining by the light of the candle. An ammunition crate stood just next to it, so the rat couldn't dodge to the left. Hook stamped his foot just to the right of the rat, making it flinch to the left and up against the ammunition crate. A quick jab and he had it.

The second rat had been pure luck. Hook had no idea there was another one further beneath the bunk. Not that he was going to tell Thompson that.

The major looked at him with something close to awe. Hook resisted the urge to shake his head in despair. Thompson was a highly decorated officer with numerous victorious raids to his credit. If he spent half the effort and ingenuity trying to get rid of his rat problem as he did giving them more German meat to gnaw on, Hook would have a serious contender, and Thompson wouldn't have so many men on the sick list.

"Now if you'll observe, sir," Hook gestured with the bayonet and skewered rats. "You will see this dugout is a study in filth."

"It's considerably cleaner than many dugouts I've seen."

"That may be true, but it still offers a veritable feast for vermin. Look, someone was eating a biscuit while sitting on the bunk. See those crumbs there? And over there is a bit of old shoe leather someone discarded while mending his boots. A rat will happily chew on that. In fact, you can see teeth marks on the edge. And we haven't even looked under the bunks yet. No doubt the men in this dugout are of the habit of sweeping any refuse under them. Out of sight, out of mind. Not for a rat, though."

Major Thompson frowned. "The men in this dugout will be coming off of sentry duty any moment now. I'll have a word with them."

Hook smiled. One-upping a superior officer, and an upper class one at that, was almost as fun as killing rats.

Heavy footsteps made them turn. Five men shambled into the dugout, looking exhausted. Hook noted that they didn't salute Thompson. He'd heard things were a bit relaxed in this particular company. Thompson certainly got results, so not even his superior officers put up much of a fuss about lax discipline. He hoped for Thompson's sake no generals from Army Command ever came on a junket through his stretch of the line, but there was little danger of that. The portly little martinets might get shot at.

"Anything to report?" Thompson asked a young man wearing sergeant's stripes.

"Crawford spotted a likely spot for that sniper's nest," the sergeant said in an accent that spoke of an Oxbridge education. "We gave the coordinates to Battery C. They said they'd give it a few shells of high explosive at midnight. Permission to go out with a section after they're done and check they got him. There's the foundation of a wall there that the artillery probably won't destroy entirely. We'll set some charges to get rid of it. Otherwise we'll just end up with another sniper."

Thompson nodded. "Do it."

Hook raised an eyebrow. An upper-class NCO, who for some reason wasn't a commissioned officer, planning a raid on his own and all but telling Thompson to approve it? Things really did work differently in the Oxs and Bucks.

A rough-looking private chimed in without so much as a by-your-leave.

"Also noticed the Huns are using that listening post near the tree stump again."

"Not in the daytime, surely," Thompson said.

"No. We spotted it because they've added some sandbags. They covered them with mud, of course, but the profile of the parapet has changed."

Thompson rubbed his chin. "We've wiped out that listening post twice. Looks like they haven't learned their lesson, or they're trying to lure us into a trap."

"Might be," one of the other privates nodded.

"Scout out the sniper's nest and destroy the wall if the RA doesn't blast it to atoms. We'll wait on the listening post. Try to get a look at it while you're out there but don't approach nearer than twenty yards. The Huns are too careful to have made a slip up like changing how their parapet looks."

The rough private looked at Hook like he was seeing him for the first time.

"Who's he?" he asked, jabbing a thumb in Hook's direction.

Thompson smiled. "Our rat catcher."

The private grabbed his hand and pumped it. "Well, it's about bloody time! The little buggers are all over me at night. I swear I got more rats on me than lice."

"Judging from the state of this trench you might be right," Hook replied.

"Oi, what you mean?" the private asked.

"I forgot to introduce you," Thompson said. "This is Private Crawford. Here's Sergeant Willoughby, and here's Corporal Fisher and Privates Black and Anderson. Men, this is the famous Sergeant Adam Hook, who has the unique distinction of being the only man in His Majesty's Armed Forces to be mentioned in dispatches for killing rats."

"That's a fine bit of work," Crawford grumbled. "I've killed a hundred Huns and never once been mentioned in dispatches."

"That's because you're a wanker," Private Black said.

Everyone laughed except for Major Thompson, who tried to suppress a smile.

"Well, I must be off to see about bringing some more cartridges up," Thompson said. "Settle in and if you need anything just ask. Oh, and men, clean this dugout. Hook says it's not up to the mark."

Thompson climbed the steps of the dugout and was gone.

Crawford looked around. "What's he on about it not being up to the mark?"

Hook turned to Crawford. "A thousand little details, let me show you."

A proper cleaning took an hour. They scoured the place for crumbs, improperly secured food, and bits of leather. Sergeant Willoughby discovered to his dismay that a cake sent to him by his mother had been attacked. Well, what did the fellow expect? He should have put a nail into one of the roof beams and hung the package from the ceiling. Private Black discovered that rats had gnawed at a cigarette packet he had foolishly hidden under his blanket, as if they wouldn't be able to sniff it out. The men also cleaned out a stash of empty wine bottles from under Crawford's bunk. These they buried in the floor of the dugout. Thompson was a bit free with the men, but there were limits.

Their work also gave them a chance to fight the rats. Hook killed two with his bayonet and stomped another that scuttled out from beneath Willoughby's pack. Crawford managed to squish one with an entrenching tool and Black chased one all the way out of the dugout and came back crowing that he'd kicked it to death.

Once they were done, they sat down for a smoke. Private Anderson, who looked like he had lied about his age to enlist, acted as jobs body and passed around some biscuits before busying himself making coffee on a small spirit stove. When the coffee was done, he passed Hook a mug. Crawford spiked it with something from his flask. The flask went around to all the men except Corporal Fisher, who turned up his nose.

"A teetotaler from the God Squad," Crawford explained. "Don't mind him, he kills Huns as good as the next man. Cheers."

"Cheers," Hook replied. Everyone clunked their coffee mugs together.

Hook took a sip of the adulterated coffee and nearly choked. This was homemade stuff or he was a Chinaman. Probably made with ditch water and fermented socks. He hoped it wouldn't make him go blind.

Anderson took a big gulp and sputtered. Everyone laughed.

"A good kid, but can't hold his liquor," Crawford said, slapping him on the back.

"Probably not allowed into his local," Hook said. "They know his age."

"I'm eighteen," Anderson said, his voice coming out choked.

"Of course you are," Hook said.

Anderson sat up straight and put on what he no doubt thought was a hard face. "I'm old enough to kill Hun."

"How many days ago did you get here?" Hook asked.

"Oh, he'll be fine," Corporal Fisher said. "This is only his second week but he's doing his duty."

Hook nodded. Fisher had the air of a veteran about him. They all did, except for Anderson. He had that panicked look of the new arrival. That fear would fade with time, or get him killed.

Hook gestured at the bunk they'd indicated was his.

"So who am I replacing?"

"Corporal Pierce," Willoughby said, making a face. "Killed two days ago by William Tell."

"William Tell?"

"That sniper we're hunting. The chaps call him that because he shot the cap right off our medical man's head. Didn't even wound him, the lucky fellow. Pierce wasn't so lucky. A week before that, William Tell got Private Stroud. Anderson was his replacement."

Hook glanced at Anderson. The lad looked like he was going to be sick.

Hook gave him a reassuring smile. "Keep your head down and you'll have nothing to fear. The artillery will probably snuff him out tonight."

"I'm glad you're here," said Private Anderson, leaning in close and dropping his voice to a whisper. "This trench is cursed."

"All trenches are cursed," Hook grunted.

Anderson shook his head. "You don't understand. It's cursed by the Rat King."

"The what?"

"The Rat King. He rules over the rats, he does, and he's as smart as a man. Smarter even."

Hook glanced at the others. Willoughby rolled his eyes, but the rest looked deadly serious. Corporal Fisher even whispered an "Our Father". Hook turned back to Anderson.

"What you on about?"

Anderson's eyes grew wide. "They took over this trench from the Frenchies last month and found the place already crawling with rats. Thompson complained about the state of things, but the Frenchies said it wasn't their fault. Their rat killer had gone mad."

"Gone mad?"

"That's what they said. It was before my time but the other lads got to talk with him. For some reason the Frenchies hadn't sent him to a sanitarium. Was still on the line but his nerves were shot."

"That much is true," Willoughby said, "but the rest is pure rubbish."

"If only it were," Black grumbled.

"So you believe this too?" Hook asked.

"I got to talk with the poor bloke," Black said. "We all did, and what he said made me weaker in the knees than I've been since I was as new as Anderson here."

"If you're pulling the new chap's leg, please stop. It will make my job that much more difficult," Hook said.

Crawford shook his head. "We don't play those games here. A nervous man is a careless man, and careless men get killed."

Hook studied his new companions. No, they weren't riding Anderson. They believed this. All except for the toff with the sergeant's stripes.

He turned to Willoughby. "So you talked with the French rat killer too?"

The sergeant nodded, looking grim.

"And what did he say?"

"His nerves were shattered. A classic case of shell shock, the poor devil. He was saying all sorts of nonsense. They all do when they crack."

"What sort of nonsense?"

"There's a man like a—" Anderson started. Hook held up a hand to stop him.

"Let your sergeant tell it."

Hook wanted to hear the story from the man who didn't believe it. These others had probably exaggerated the tale beyond all recognition.

Willoughby made a face. "Well, the chap was raving. He said that he'd found an underground lair the rats used. It wasn't just a rat hole, but a proper tunnel big enough for a man. He squeezed into it and discovered a network of rooms. And there...well...there's where the story gets queer."

"He saw a man with the hide and head of a rat," Anderson said, his voice quavering. "Ten feet tall it was, with glowing eyes—"

"It wasn't any more than six feet," Willoughby interrupted him. "The fellow said it was the size of a man, not a giant. And he made no mention of glowing eyes."

"I heard its eyes glow."

"You weren't even there."

Anderson's face paled. "But I've seen them. While on sentry duty I've seen the eyes at night, shining far out in No Man's Land. Looking at me."

Willoughby scowled. "It was probably a pair of Huns enjoying a fag. You should have fired at them."

"So where was this tunnel he found?" Hook asked.

"He wasn't clear. He said this Rat King chased him and he fled. He managed to collapse the tunnel behind him and get away."

"That won't stop the Rat King," Fisher said. "It's the Devil, sure as I'm a Christian. If the little rats can burrow through mud and clay, imagine what some diabolical Rat King could do."

Hook gave an annoyed sigh. "I've been hunting rats for two years now. If there was a Rat King, I'd know it."

Crawford leveled his gaze at him. "You've never been to this stretch of line before. You said yourself you've never seen so many rats. Maybe this is the Rat King's court. And while you may not know about him, he probably knows about you."

A chill went down Hook's spine. It was ridiculous, pure superstition, but the rats did seem to know him. He'd been attacked more than once. Rats were clever creatures. Maybe after having killed so many of their kind, they really did sense he was their enemy. But a Rat King? No.

Willoughby's reasonable voice cut in.

"We searched for the tunnel, of course. The man was mad but he could have stumbled upon a tunnel the Huns were digging. We found nothing."

"The Rat King has hidden it," Black said, his eyes wide.

"Don't be daft," Willoughby said.

The dugout fell into an uncomfortable silence. Hook took another gulp of his spiked coffee. He hoped Crawford would offer him some more before he turned in.

***

Hook stood in No Man's Land. A low mist clung to the ground, coiling around the English and German corpses and settling in the craters to make little pools of gray vapor. All was silent. No flares shot overhead and no guns fired. The dead lay still, yet they moved.

Rats were swarming over them. They went for the soft parts first—the eyes and ears and nose. Or they dug through the men's trousers to gnaw on the other soft parts within. The rats working on corpses that had been out for a time, that had already lost the soft bits, tore at the legs and arms and cheeks.

It wasn't long before the whole body would be stripped. Some rats would burrow right inside, their heads poking out of large holes in the belly, eyes glittering as they scanned the wasteland for fresher prey.

A low groan emanated from the dead.

Hook looked around.

"Lawson?" he called out.

The groan came again, cutting through the mist. Hook scanned the carpet of bodies.

"Lawson?" he called again.

Derrick Lawson had been his pal. They'd grown up together, enlisted together. He was out here somewhere, hurt. Hook needed to find him.

"Lawson?"

"Hook." The mist carried the soft moan of his name to his ears.

Hook spun around. His friend staggered towards him. Lawson's eyes were empty sockets, his cheeks and ears torn away. His trousers had been rent open and although he tried not to look, Hook saw that his friend's private parts had been consumed.

"You left me, Hook. You left me to be eaten."

The corpse's gnawed lips barely moved. Hook stood rooted to the spot, paralyzed with fear.

"Ho—" Lawson's voice choked off. He worked his lips, trying to say more, but no sound came out except a gagging cough. His mouth opened wider. Lawson choked again, and a bewhiskered snout appeared from his mouth. Glittering little eyes fixed Hook with an evil stare.

Lawson choked again and the rat jumped from his mouth. Another followed, and another. A rat dropped from his pants. Lawson lurched, his belly distending. With a loud tearing sound it burst open and a cluster of rats heaved forth.

They came straight for Hook.

Hook woke with a start. A lone candle flickered at the table. Anderson was sitting there sewing a patch on his spare shirt. He looked up at Hook.

"You all right?" he asked.

Hook nodded, not trusting himself to speak.

"Bad dream?"

Hook shrugged.

"I get them sometimes too. Nerves. You'll be fine in the morning."

Hook grunted and turned his back on him. Who did this raw recruit think he was, talking to him like a veteran? He closed his eyes and tried to relax.

The dream was always the same, most of the details torn from unforgettable reality. It had been a year ago, in early 1915. Their regiment had charged the German line and got mowed down by

Maxims and Mausers. Men had writhed and fallen all around. Lawson had been right beside him and took a bullet in the gut. Hook stopped to help his pal but the major had ordered him forward. Always forward, never stop for an injured man. That was the army's motto. When Hook protested, the major leveled his Webley at him. Hook gave his friend one last look and headed towards the German line.

The attack was a disaster, as usual. In the chaos of the retreat, Hook hadn't been able to find his friend.

Hook did find the major, though, shot through the head and staring blankly at the smoke-filled sky. That had given him a bit of satisfaction.

He found Lawson the following week while on night patrol. His friend's face and genitals had been eaten, just like in his dream. They'd found him not on the flat, exposed area where Hook had been forced to leave him, but in a shell crater. There was a field dressing around his middle, although the rats had chewed through that. Lawson's canteen lay not far off and gripped in one hand was the crushed body of a rat.

Lawson had survived long enough to get to shelter and dress his wound. He'd lived long enough to have a drink of water and wonder why his best friend had abandoned him. He'd lived long enough for the rats to close in. They could sense weakness and would go after a man if they thought he couldn't defend himself.

But Lawson had defended himself. With the last of his strength he'd fought off the vermin as they crawled all over him, their teeth sinking into his flesh. He'd crushed one before the rat bites made him pass out with blood loss and terror.

Hook shuddered and wiped his eyes.

I'm sorry, Lawson. I am so sorry.

Sleep took a long time to come.

***

The next day was one of the most amusing of Hook's young life. He'd never seen such blundering. The Oxs and Bucks may be good at killing Germans, but they proved useless at killing rats.

The men were in high spirits because the artillery had blasted the sniper's nest, and Willoughby's night patrol had destroyed any remaining cover and came back reporting they'd found the William Tell's body parts strewn all over the crater. Everyone felt buoyant at having avenged the death of so many comrades. This got them in fighting spirits for the competition.

Assuming the comedy show Hook witnessed could be called a competition. Men rushed back and forth in the trench, chasing rats with bayonets and entrenching tools. Others sought out rat holes and tried to smoke them out, waiting with one booted foot raised to stamp on the occupants when they emerged.

This didn't work, of course, because every rat burrow has at least two exits. The smoke did help Hook explore the network, though. A man would light a fire with kindling taken from a broken up ammunition crate and blow the smoke into the hole, and Hook would see the smoke issue from another hole ten feet down the line. Using a periscope borrowed from Sergeant Willoughby, he scanned No Man's Land and saw several wisps of smoke rising up, followed by the rats. The Oxs and Bucks were making far too much noise in the trench for the rats to emerge anywhere inside. As he looked he spotted a periscope poking up from the German line. Lord knew what the Huns thought of all these goings-on.

Some men tried to get clever. Fisher lived up to his name by finding a rat hole, and instead of lighting a fire he shoved a length of barbed wire up it. When he pulled it out it came covered with tufts of fur and blood, but the rats had made their escape.

Willoughby devised an ingenious trap involving springs, wire, and several bayonets, but Major Thompson made him disassemble it when he almost lost a foot.

By the end of the day the men were exhausted and dispirited. Private Black was the winner with a miserable total of seven rats killed. Crawford was the runner up with five. Most men hadn't caught a one.

Hook stood beside a sour-faced Major Thompson and lectured the men on what they'd done wrong. Then he showed them how to do things right. Stabbing and smashing were all well and good if done with a bit of stealth, but you'd never tip the balance that way. You needed traps. Hook explained about poisons and box traps and his own inventions such as The Fricassee and The Rat Splat, and then pointed out the best spots to lay them. He ended his lecture by explaining that fumigation techniques would never work because of the way rat warrens were made.

He ordered a man to build a fire in front of one of the rat holes. Once the flames got going and the man was puffing the smoke into the hole, Hook lifted the periscope and scanned No Man's Land.

"All right, so all the smoke's going into the hole," Hook said. "But looking out there I can see three plumes of smoke coming up. I see rats coming out too. Just to the right and a little further out I see a line of smoke, which is a bit strange. Must be a crack in the earth from all the shelling. That smoke you're making is pushing them out of the trench but once the smoke's gone they'll come right back in. Now if you'll each step up to the periscope..."

Before Hook could take his eyes from the viewer there was the sharp crack of a rifle shot and the periscope bucked, hitting the trench wall and bouncing back to smack him in the face.

Hook stumbled off the fire step.

"What the hell?"

He blinked and looked at the periscope lying at his feet. The top mirror had been smashed and a neat bullet hole punctured the back.

"That was William Tell! The bugger's not dead," Crawford said.

"I thought you said the artillery killed him," Hook said, holding his face. He was going to end up with two black eyes.

"The artillery killed *a* sniper. Looks like they didn't get *the* sniper," Crawford replied.

"How can you know it was him?"

"His rifle is a special model," Willoughby explained. "Something new. I don't know what the Germans call it but it has a distinct sound. It's surely him."

"Looks like we have some more hunting to do," Black said.

"And I'll get to work on your rat problem," Hooked said, rubbing his eyes.

Thompson gave him five men to help, led by Corporal Fisher and including young Private Anderson. For the rest of the day Hook constructed and set his traps. He also trained the men how to attack suddenly. Rats could sense danger, and if you rushed at them they would scamper away. In the cramped interior of the trenches, with men having to squeeze around equipment and other men, all the while struggling with mud, a rat could easily outrun its hunter. The only way to get one was to lash out suddenly and hit the first time.

Luckily the men were quick studies. By the end of the day they had strings of vermin to show off to their commander. Hook had to stop the men from throwing them over the parapet. This had been their custom, the fools not realizing that doing so only provided more food for the surviving rats. Instead he had them collected in bags and dumped far to the rear in an unoccupied stretch of countryside.

By the end of the day Hook was equal parts satisfied and frustrated. The training had gone well, several traps were laid, and they'd bagged a couple of hundred rats, but there seemed to be just as many as before. In fact, there seemed to be more. When he mentioned this Anderson muttered fearfully under his breath and Fisher prayed.

Fools. Hook decided to turn in and start fresh in the morning.

***

Hook woke with a start. He'd had that dream again.

The dugout was pitch black yet he could still almost see Lawson beckoning to him with his chewed face, asking why he'd left him in No Man's Land.

It was a dream. You're awake now. Everything is fine.

The snores of his bunkmates reassured him. In the distance he heard the low thudding of artillery fire. Neither of these had woken him. What had caught his attention was a softer sound, inaudible but for his trained ears.

A scratching, scrabbling sound.

Rats, and a hell of a lot of them.

Hook tried to slow his breathing and relax his muscles. Rats, just rats. That was all. His head rested on a spare set of clothes he had bundled up for a pillow. Underneath, as always, was his knife. As quietly as he could, he eased his hand beneath the pillow and grabbed the hilt. His breath caught and his hand froze as he heard a scrabbling close by. A soft squeak came from somewhere in the darkness. They were close.

Rats, only rats. But why so many? He had killed all the ones in the dugout and stopped up a rat hole he'd found. He and the men had gone through this place so well that it was the cleanest spot on the Western Front. Of course rats could have found their way in, they always did, but why here?

Hook remembered his greatcoat hung on the side of the bunk. In his pocket was a box of matches. Gripping his knife in one hand, he reached out with the other. He touched the thick, damp wool. Running his hand down, he found his pocket and reached inside.

His fingers touched rough fur. Teeth latched onto his forefinger.

Hook flew out of bed with a howl and landed hard on the floor. The rat held fast to his finger. He slapped his hand down on the floor once, twice, three times, and the beast let go. A soft, fat body scuttled up his leg. He batted it aside just as another passed over his shoulder.

He screamed again as teeth clamped on his neck. He tore off the rat and flung it into the darkness.

A light flared up. Anderson's shocked face was illuminated in a halo of match light. In the next bunk, Fisher untangled himself from his blankets and grabbed his rifle.

Hook looked around wildly. Rats scuttled everywhere, fleeing the sudden light. Hook slashed with his knife and cut the nearest in half. He leapt on another and stabbed it through its bloated stomach, no doubt filled with the corpse flesh of some dead Tommy.

"Shoot them! Shoot them!" he heard himself cry. "They attacked me!"

"The Rat King!" Anderson wailed.

"Where?" Hook demanded. He looked around, but saw only rats and the dim interior of the dugout.

Wait, what was that over there? It looked like a man but with brown hide. It stood almost five feet tall right in the corner of the room. Hook screamed again and snatched up a nearby rifle.

And then the match went out.

Hook released the safety, aimed at where he remembered the figure to be, and let loose. In the flare of the muzzle he saw it. He fired again, and for another instant saw the strange figure, so brown, so manlike yet so unlike a man. Someone shouted. The gunshots drowned out the words as Hook kept firing until another match illuminated the room...

...and he saw before him the bullet-riddled greatcoat of Colonel Fisher hanging on a hook.

***

Hook avoided his bunkmates the next day, mortified by his cowardly behavior. He made his rounds to empty his traps and busied himself making more. Every now and then he lashed out with his bayonet and skewered another rat.

Even that didn't make him feel better. He'd made a fool of himself last night. Even worse, Anderson kept coming up to him and asking if he was all right, or if he needed something. While the kid was only trying to help, it felt humiliating.

Something else bothered him too—that line of smoke he'd seen the day before. At first he'd shrugged it off as a crack in the ground. Thinking on it again, he realized that didn't make sense. The ground was too muddy to crack. It would just cave in. Even the rats had to constantly dig out their burrows to keep them from collapsing. The spoil from their excavations was one of the best ways to find the openings.

So if that hadn't been a crack, what had it been? It was obviously connected with the burrow the chaps of the Oxs and Bucks had been trying to smoke out, but rats made small, inconspicuous openings, not large cuts in the ground. Judging from the smoke, it had been a yard long. Even stranger, it had been a good twenty yards away from the trench. If their burrow was that large, it was the largest he'd ever seen, and he'd seen quite a few.

Curious, he returned to the stretch of trench where the man had first lit the fire. The burrow had been blocked with a stone and some old sacking. Hook cleared it out, got some tinder from a cook in one of the support trenches, and started a small fire.

Sergeant Willoughby came up to him. "We really shouldn't be lighting unnecessary fires. It gets the Huns' wind up. Likely to attract a mortar round or two."

"This is necessary," Hook said, not turning away from his work. "Do you have a periscope?"

"I'll fetch one."

Willoughby returned a minute later with a periscope. It had been daubed with mud and was camouflaged on its top end with twigs. Hook noticed a bullet hole on the top.

"Yes, it's the same as yesterday. Crawford fixed it. Hope you're not superstitious," Willoughby laughed.

Hook scowled at him. "What makes you say that?"

"Oh, sorry, it's just that you got this one shot out of your hands only yesterday. Some chaps get queer about such things. I didn't mean anything," Willoughby said, obviously flustered.

"Never mind," Hook said. It was strange that this veteran could so easily be made uncomfortable. Willoughby talked about sneaking into No Man's Land as if he was going punting but got out of sorts at the least sign of disapproval. An odd bunch, this Company E.

"I'll go to the next fire bay and give you cover," Willoughby said.

"What for?"

"If I give the Hun a few rounds it will keep their heads down. Then you can put the periscope up. When they next look over their parapet, they'll be looking at my fire bay, not yours. It will make them less likely to spot your periscope."

Hook nodded. He turned to the nearest private to order him to tend the fire and make sure the smoke was going in the hole, but the man was already doing it.

They're an odd bunch, but a game one.

Willoughby disappeared around the traverse. Hook waited. After a minute, a few shots snapped from the next fire bay. He eased the periscope up and took a look.

Yes, there it was. A thin curtain of smoke rising in a line a yard long. What was that? It certainly wasn't a rat burrow, although the rats were using it. He could see the little devils issuing forth from it to escape the smoke.

"See what you want?" Willoughby's voice came from behind him.

"You got back quick."

"Didn't want William Tell replying in kind."

"Take a look at this."

Willoughby stared through the periscope for a minute.

"Do you mean that line of smoke?"

"Exactly. At first I thought it was a crack in the earth, but the ground is too muddy for that. Rats don't make such big openings for their burrows, so what could it be?"

Willoughby pulled the periscope down below the parapet and smiled. "Perhaps it's the Rat King's front door."

The man fanning the smoke gasped. "Don't say that! You might attract his attention!"

Willoughby laughed. Hook shifted from one foot to the other, trying to hide his uneasiness.

"You can put that fire out," Hook told the private, "We're done."

"So what do you think it is?" Willoughby said.

"I don't know. Perhaps a cellar?"

"There was no house there, I don't think. We would have at least seen a few bricks. There are a couple of other ruins scattered about No Man's Land like the one we destroyed the other night, and they are all visible enough."

Hook thought for a moment. Before he could form his thoughts into something coherent, the private spoke up. "It's the Rat King's burrow, I tell you. You said yourself you saw a heap of rats coming out of there, and it weren't made by rats. I bet the Rat King has a burrow as big as a mineshaft to hide in and rule over his kingdom."

"Quite a kingdom," Willoughby laughed.

"Perhaps it is a mineshaft," Hook said, not wanting to think of the alternative. "Perhaps the Germans were digging a sap and came up too soon."

Willoughby considered that for a moment. "Perhaps. If that were the case, we'd need to have a look. They might decide to redirect it. It's already most of the way to our line. I doubt they'd let all that work go to waste."

"Who's to say they have? They might still be there," Hook said.

Willoughby nodded. "Looks like I'll have to lead another party into No Man's Land tonight."

Hook tried to speak. It took him a moment to get the words out. "I want to be on it. If there's something...something the rats have out there, I'll need to see it."

Hook turned away before he saw what kind of look Willoughby gave him.

***

Going over the top was the hardest part. Hook had made his share of charges into machine gun fire, every veteran had, and he knew from bitter experience that climbing out of the relative safety of the trench and into death-laden open air was the toughest thing a man could do.

It turned out the same held true for creeping out on a night scout.

Willoughby was in command so he went first. He slithered out over the parapet through a light rain and wormed his way forward under a stretch of wire that had been left a bit high for the purpose. Crawford went next, followed by Anderson. Then it was his turn. Fisher took up the rear.

Hook tried not to think about that sniper as he crept up the ladder and got on his belly. He could just see Anderson and Crawford in the murk ahead. He crawled forward, wincing at every squish of the mud. He hoped the rain would mask the sound.

Far to the south, the sky flashed and boomed to the firing of distant guns. They were so far away Hook wasn't sure if they were British or German. There had been some scattered firing in this sector just after dark, but nothing for some time. It was now midnight.

The still, silent air felt heavy with menace. William Tell was out there, Hook felt sure. And he knew that the Germans would be watching. That listening post they'd reoccupied stuck far out into No Man's Land, getting to within a hundred yards of their destination. The land around the mysterious crack was relatively flat and with few major craters. If the scouting party was spotted, they'd be far too exposed.

Hook tried not to think about it. He got under the first line of wire with no trouble and angled a few yards to the right like he had been told in order to make his way to a small opening in the second line of wire.

Anderson waited for him there. The lad spotted him and without a word turned and headed further into No Man's Land. Hook glanced back to make sure Fisher was behind him, and then followed Anderson.

A few yards beyond the second line of wire was their first rendezvous point—a shell crater where at the lip a weathered skeleton, its bones whitened by time and held together only by a few tendons, made a good landmark. Hook spotted it ahead. In the flickering light of the distant artillery barrage he could make out the distinctive ridged crest of an Adrian helmet, showing the man to be French.

Briefly he wondered how long the poor bastard had been lying out here. This patch of ground had been fought over since 1914. Dismissing that thought as irrelevant and distracting—nobody wanted to be distracted on a night patrol—he slid into the crater and right on top of Crawford.

The loudmouth didn't utter a word. Hook could barely make out Willoughby and Anderson beside him, lying still so as to not make any unnecessary noise. He sensed more than heard Fisher ease into the crater beside him.

They lay still for five minutes. Due to his job, Hook hadn't been on many patrols into No Man's Land, but he knew this was standard procedure. There was no way five men could go over the top and get it this far out without making some noise. It was best to be silent for a time to allay suspicion. He knew from his own sentry duties that No Man's Land was filled with frightening sounds—squishes, rustles, creaks, the occasional moan. They could be rats or birds or some wounded man stranded out between the lines. They could be the wind or the rain, or soil subsiding down the side of a crater. Or they could be a raiding party coming to kill you.

A sentry couldn't fire at every sound or launch a flare every time he thought a shadow moved. That would bring enemy fire, or at least a good talking to by the platoon commander. No, one had to be as quiet on sentry duty as one was on patrol.

The Germans knew this too. He imagined some wide-eyed Teuton staring out into the darkness, perhaps gazing right at their position, not seeing it but wondering if the sounds he'd heard from that direction were something to worry about. Wait a little and his attention would be distracted by other sounds, other phantom movements. Then would be the time to move again.

He felt someone's hand touch his own. That time was now.

Hook's heart was thumping, but he felt no real fear. Two years in the trenches had pounded that out of him. Instead he felt a heightened awareness, a tense connection with everything around him.

The only anomaly to that were his night terrors. While he was not alone in having them, they had gotten worse since he had come to this part of the line.

Willoughby headed out, moving forward and to the right towards the position of the mysterious crack. At least Hook assumed the figure was Willoughby. It could have been Hook's own mother and he wouldn't have recognized that dark form, that slight deepening of the shadows, as the woman who had raised him. Hook waited until the third man had gone by and took his place. He wondered if everyone had kept their order. Knowing how good Company E was, he bet they had.

They passed around another crater and came to a flat stretch. Hook guessed they were close.

Suddenly the sky lit up as a flare sputtered up from the German lines.

Everyone froze. To hit the dirt would bring the bullets. Movement was easier to spot in the flickering light and shadows than a strange shape. Hook went rigid, halfway through bringing one hand and leg forward.

The flare rose up a bit to the north of their position. Hook didn't dare turn his head to look at what lay in that direction.

Several rifles barked further down the line. What were they shooting at? Willoughby had said there were no other patrols out at this time. Were the Germans panicking at a false alarm? Had they gotten spooked by one of their own patrols?

Moving only his eyes, Hook studied the terrain in front. Past the three men ahead of him he could see a flat area about a quarter the size of a football pitch. Near its center, a straight shadow about a yard long cut a pitch black line across the ground. One side looked rounded, while the other appeared to be eroded away. He averted his eyes to see better, but the light of the flare after half a night of darkness dazzled him. All he could tell was that they were approaching what they sought. What that was, he still had no idea.

The flare rose to its apex and started to fall, winking out as it did. Hook let out his breath. He could almost hear the others in the patrol tense as his lungs emptied in an audible gust.

He'd get it from Crawford once they got back to the line. If they got back to the line.

Nobody moved. Hook allowed himself to sink quietly to the earth. He could just make out the bottom of Anderson's boot in front of him. After about a minute that boot moved forward.

Hook started to crawl, trying to keep as quiet as these men, who were obviously far more comfortable in No Man's Land than he was. Company E was legendary. People said they practically lived out here. All except for Anderson, of course, but even he was less of a student at these things than Hook. A couple of weeks with Company E were worth two years in a regular unit.

Carried about the same risk, too. All those commendations hadn't come without a price.

Anderson's boots came into view again, as did those of another man. Hook crawled up between them and found his companions staring at a dark line in the shadows. The distant artillery barrage flickered to a greater intensity, and Hook caught a glimpse of the crack cutting through a surface slightly lighter in hue than the surrounding mud.

Something scampered over his right hand. Hook flinched and flicked it away.

Hook peered at the crack but could see nothing. He reached out and pressed on the shoulders of the men to either side of him. They moved back to give him room. A third shadow moved to his left. His fourth companion, presumably Fisher, was hanging back, although Hook had no idea where.

Now that he had room to maneuver, Hook made a circuit of the crack.

Another rat scurried over his arm He shuddered, elbowed it to one side, and drew his bayonet. He caught a glimpse of a rat close to his face and lashed out. His quick reflexes were rewarded with a plaintive squeak. He wiped the thing off the end of his bayonet and felt around the crack.

It felt like hewn masonry, not brick like you typically find in cellars. The side facing the British trench was eroded away for about a foot and he could feel the curve of a roof. His fingers found a seam between two hewn blocks. This was manmade and the rough handiwork gave the impression of great age.

Crawling along, he felt the curve of the masonry continue until it was buried under a heap of soil. Running along the top of the curve was an eroded portion, broken through by the weather or something else, he couldn't tell. The crack was just wide enough to squeeze through.

The thought of doing that made him shiver, yet that was the mission. If this led to some old wine cellar of some forgotten manor house, or the basement of a disappeared farm, who knew where it may lead from there? The Germans might have discovered it too. He and his patrol had to find out.

Hook swiped at another rat but only managed to wound it. It scurried away, squeaking loudly.

He glanced at his companions huddled not far away. Although it was too dark to pick out individual faces, their tense pose expressed impatience and disapproval. Killing rats was too noisy of a job for No Man's Land.

Continuing his circuit of the crack and exposed masonry, he pushed away more rats. They seemed to be everywhere. He resisted the urge to stab them and studied the opening.

The ground was more eroded on the German side. In fact the crack wasn't at the apex of the arch or vault or whatever he was probing, but slightly below and facing the enemy trench.

Hook pressed his cheek against the damp mud, looking towards the German trench from the level of the crack. The sky shimmered with the faint light of the distant artillery bombardment, and he could see the darker outline of the ground silhouetted against it. There was a slight rise between the German trench and where he lay. That meant the crack wasn't visible from their lines. Good. To the left, however, the land dipped and became more exposed. That's where the sniper and the observation post lay. While he didn't think they'd be able to make out the crack even in daytime, there wasn't enough terrain to hide the patrol in case the enemy decided to send up another flare.

The best thing to do was to get into the thing and out of sight. It was their job in any case, so it wasn't like they had a choice.

He crawled back to the patrol to find them in a whispered argument.

"What's wrong?" he asked.

"Anderson and Fisher don't want to go down, the bloody fools," Willoughby hissed.

"This isn't the House of Commons, order them," Hook said.

Willoughby hesitated. Hook was about to order them himself when Willoughby whispered, "Come on lads, this needs to be done."

Anderson's quavering voice came out of the darkness, "What if the Rat King—"

"Keep your bally voice down," Hook whispered.

Someone pushed someone else, Hook guessed it was Crawford pushing Anderson, and the group moved to the crack with Hook and Willoughby at the front. One of the party lingered back. Hook thought it was Fisher. Willoughby made an impatient gesture and the lingerer crawled forward.

A rifle shot shattered the still night air.

Everyone got down. That had been close. Hook tried to make himself flat as possible and waited for the next bullet to come. It didn't. They'd need to stay still and quiet for a time before they could go to the opening. Even though it lay barely two yards away, they couldn't risk the noise.

Hook felt a small weight on his ankle. The rat scuttled up his leg, its claws pricking him through his trousers, and got up on his back. It was joined by a second rat that scurried up his side. Both rats paused in the small of his back. Hook gritted his teeth. Then the rats flashed down to the back of his head. One sank its fangs into his ear.

Hook cried out and rolled over. The rifle cracked again. After a moment, someone else shouted. Had the sniper hit? It sounded more like surprise than agony. Perhaps the rats had found another victim.

The rifle fired again, this time spitting up a clod of earth inches from Hook's head.

"Get in the opening before they send up a flare," Willoughby whispered.

That was all the encouragement Hook needed. He slithered over the mud and wasted a valuable second turning around. While he feared the sniper more than the rats, there was no way he was going to go into that vault head first.

As he squeezed his body through the opening, his elbow broke off a piece of stone that clattered loudly onto a stone surface just below his feet. That set off another shot from William Tell. Hook let go and dropped.

His feet landed on smooth stone a short way down. The sky was a dark gray band just above his head.

Anderson's voice came down from above, far too loud, "I don't want to!"

The band of sky was blocked for a moment. Hook had just enough time to step to the side before a body fell to the floor beside him.

"Oh God!" Anderson moaned from beside him.

There was a distant hiss, and bright white light shone through the opening above their heads. The Germans had sent up another flare. The sniper's rifle fired three times in rapid succession before being drowned out by the loud rattle of a Maxim.

Hook stared at the crack, hoping to hear a shout or cry from the rest of the patrol, or to see someone crawling inside, but there was no sign of them. As the flare reached its apex Hook looked away to keep from being dazzled, and saw for the first time where he had landed.

They stood in the center of a vaulted room about six feet high, ten wide, and fifteen long. A portal at one end led into darkness. There was nothing in the room except rats, rats everywhere—scampering around the floor, climbing the walls, sitting on the edge of the crack and looking down at them with glittering eyes. Hook gaped. There must have been hundreds of them. Never in all his career as a rat killer had he ever seen so many in one place.

A strangled cry made him turn. Anderson stood next to him, body shaking and eyes wide. He was kicking at any rat nearby while fumbling to get his rifle unslung.

Hook put his hands on the lad's shoulders. "Calm down. It's all right. We're a sight better safer down here than up there."

As if to emphasize his point, the Maxim let off another burst. Anderson jerked his chin upwards. "Oh God, the others!"

"Keep your voice down. Either they're safe or they aren't and there's nothing we can do about it."

Anderson jerked and kicked. A rat went flying.

"Calm down," Hook whispered. He felt a rat climb his own leg and kicked too.

With shaking hands, Anderson unslung his rifle and was about to pull back the bolt when Hook slapped him. Anderson sucked in breath and gaped at Hook.

"Enough already," Hook said, kicking off another rat, "Keep your wits about you and let's see what's here. That's what we came for, remember?"

"I know what's here, it's the—"

"You say it's the bloody Rat King and I'll slap you again, you fucking idiot."

Anderson bit his lower lip. Hook unslung his own rifle and fixed the bayonet. The flare was descending now, and the shimmering light coming from the crack was beginning to dim. Hook jabbed at a couple of rats nearby. Anderson stomped one and impaled another.

"Beastly things," the young man said.

"Got a lighter?" Hook asked.

"Yes."

"Sling your rifle and light it. We'll have no light soon."

"Sling my rifle?"

"That's an order. I'll kill the rats, you help me see. Besides, in the state you're in I don't want you blasting away and waking every Hun from here to Berlin."

Anderson slung his rifle, pulled a lighter out of his pocket, and lit it. A rat fell from the crack onto his shoulder and he cried out, dropping the lighter. By the last light of the flare, Hook retrieved it and handed it back to him.

"They're only rats," Hook told him, trying to keep his voice even.

"It bit me!"

"I've been bitten twice already. Now keep your voice down."

The illumination from the lighter was dimmer than the flare but steadier. The rats seemed afraid of it too, clearing a circle around them and glaring at them with hateful eyes filled with reflected flame. Hook gestured towards the doorway. Anderson gulped and followed him.

Hook kept his rifle level. His heart beat madly in his chest, and he told himself it was only because of the danger of Germans, not the rats. As they approached the doorway, he could see it led to another room identical to the one they'd entered.

"Bloody hell, it's like an underground palace," Anderson whispered.

"More likely an old crypt for some chateau or church that disappeared before the war. This place probably dates to the Middle Ages. Reminds me of some of the crypts under the old churches back home."

Anderson let out a worried sigh.

"Oh, you're not scared of ghosts too, are you?" Hook grumbled.

"N-no. It's the Rat—"

"Oh Jesus, do shut up."

The second room was as empty as the first except for the rats, which scurried about in their hundreds. Hook's skin prickled. How could there be so many? What did they eat? Why weren't they up top, where there was meat to be had in plenty? While it was warmer and drier here, rats didn't much care about such things. It made no sense.

Hook saw the dark opening of a doorway at the end of the second room.

"Follow me," he said.

Anderson hesitated, holding the lighter high and looked around with bugged-out eyes.

"I-I don't want to."

"That's an order. Move."

Hook jabbed a rat out of spite and stepped forward. The circle of light didn't follow him. As he got close to the edge of the shadows, the rats crept towards him.

"Come on!" Hook called over his shoulder.

Anderson snapped out of it and took some shaky steps forward. As the light grew around Hook, the rats moved off.

Hook made it to the doorway. The room beyond was bigger than the previous two. He couldn't see well but he thought he discerned a row of several low, rectangular shapes on the floor by the far wall. Anderson reached his arm over Hook's shoulder and lit up the room.

The place teemed with rats. They covered every horizontal surface. Beneath them Hook could see a dozen rectangular slabs of what he guessed to be stone, but he couldn't say for sure. The rats were heaped two or three thick upon them, crawling all over each other like a squeaking, scrabbling carpet. Only one shape was visible beneath that roiling mass—that of a man lying amid the multitudes of rats.

Hook's breath caught. An instant later Anderson spotted it and screamed.

"The Rat King!"

Anderson dropped his lighter and bolted. As the lighter fell to the ground it flared up and for a moment the room was lit clearly enough that Hook could see the manlike shape was the bas relief of a knight carved onto the top of a sarcophagus. Then the lighter hit the floor and went out.

"It's a grave, you bloody fool. Come—"

Hook's words cut off as he heard a loud scrabbling of thousands of little claws on stone. A moment later they were streaming up both his legs. He screamed and kicked, jabbed out with his bayonet, but there were far too many. For every one he shook off, three replaced it. They swarmed up his chest and arms. Hook turned and ran, dropping his rifle as he batted at them to keep them off his head. They gnawed at him, fangs sinking into his clothing and finding the fresh meat beneath. Others bit his hands as he pushed them off. He jerked and yelped, slammed into a wall, crushing at least a dozen on his back.

They were getting onto his face and hair. One burrowed under his collar to bite him in the neck. Others tore through his shirt and made their way inside. Hook flailed and whimpered, choking off when a rat shoved itself into his mouth. He gagged and coughed the thing out, only to have another bite him on his lips. He slapped one off his forehead with a bloody hand and saw the flame of a lighter far ahead. He stumbled towards the light...

Private Anderson trembled beneath the meagre light of the crack. The flare was gone now and the screams he heard from the next room made him piss his pants. The Rat King was eating poor Hook.

A sound from above made him yelp and nearly discharge his rifle.

"Watch it!" Crawford's voice came from the murk.

He dropped to the floor, followed quickly by the other two men in the patrol.

"That was a close scrape," Crawford said, pulling out a lighter and igniting it. "Bloody. Hell."

Crawford, Willoughby, and Fisher stared at the sight of the rats all around. A scream from beyond the doorway made them spin around.

"What's happening to Hook?" Willoughby demanded.

Anderson stuttered and whimpered, unable to answer his question. If they had seen what he had seen...

...and then they did. For there in the doorway stood the Rat King. The tales had been wrong, it wasn't a rat the size of a man, it was a collection of rats taking the form of a man—a horrid, unnatural sight, an abomination. The thing wailed like a Banshee and flailed its arms, each made up of countless rodents.

"Great Scott, it's all true!" Willoughby screamed and fired at the thing. He racked the bolt back and fired again. The Rat King bucked and staggered. Rats flew off in all directions, scurrying away to reveal the stunned figure of Sergeant Hook, the famous rat killer of the Western Front. His clothing was torn, his shirt and trousers soaked with blood. His hands and face were a mass of wounds. One eye was gone. The other bugged out, wild with terror and pain. It stared at Willoughby for a moment, pleading, and then rolled up in its socket.

The rat killer fell flat on his face, dead.

CALL OF NATURE

Private Howard Black couldn't hold it in any longer.

He lay in his dugout, warm and reasonably dry. His watch told him he wouldn't be on sentry duty for another three hours. Three more hours of precious sleep. After hauling ammunition crates up from the support trenches and then standing watch all night hoping a German raiding party didn't come swarming over the parapet to slit his throat, he'd earned some sleep.

Instead, his bladder was the size of a football and he'd never catch a wink until he relieved himself.

Black couldn't do it in the dugout. It may be infested with rats and lice but adding piss to it would get Crawford and Willoughby slitting his throat quicker than the Germans. He was tempted to step out and have a quick squirt in the trench but the officers had come down hard on that. The latest to get caught was Fisher, of all people. A teetotaling religious nutter who didn't swear and thought Sunday trains were proof of Original Sin, standing there spraying the side of the trench like some Saturday night pisshead staggering home from the pub. The things war does to a man. Fisher got two weeks fatigue duty for that little stunt.

That left the latrine, a good five minutes' walk away. Black hoped he'd make it.

He groaned and rose from the slat of rotten wood that passed for his bunk. At the last minute he grabbed his Lee-Enfield rifle and gas mask. The Germans had attacked three times in the past week and only a madman went anywhere without their equipment. A few days ago Black's regiment had even been pushed out of this trench and the support trench behind it. A counterattack had regained their old quarters, but at the cost of far too many friends killed.

"Fucking Fritz," Black muttered.

He emerged into the trench, squeezing past a work crew bringing up a bale of barbed wire. That meant a trip into No Man's Land tonight. He hoped he wasn't going along.

His boots made a hollow clomp as he hurried along the duckboarding, skidding once when he hit a patch of slick mud. At least it wasn't raining today. Not too much firing either. Just the big guns launching heavy shells far overhead to land who-knew-where behind the lines, and the occasional spattering of rifle fire as British and Germans tried their best to kill one another.

He passed a machine gun emplacement and the gunner gave him a wave.

"Hey, Black, aren't you supposed to be asleep?"

"Wish I was, you bastard," Black grumbled.

The man's laughter followed him as he turned a corner into a communication trench leading for the rear. Black picked up the pace. He felt fit to burst. Why is it that you always have to piss the most just before you get to?

Another hundred yards and he came to the latrine, a little shelter of logs and compacted earth covering a deep pit. A wooden bench with a couple of holes in it acted as a seat. The wood looked damp but Black decided to sit anyway. He'd just gotten over dysentery and he daren't risk browning his trousers as he pissed.

Black pulled down his pants and made a face as he sat down. Yes, it was damp. Most of this lot couldn't shoot straight with anything other than a rifle.

A moment later it didn't matter. A feeling of profound relief came over him as he felt his bladder empty. He could hear the hot stream trickling onto the unspeakable mess a few feet below.

Black pulled his shirt over his nose. That mess needed some burying. Regulations dictated that each man had to throw lime over their business once they were done, but when was the last time a work party brought up bags of lime? With all the German assaults, the men on the firing line were lucky to get their meals.

In the dim interior of the latrine he saw a small black shape scoot past. A rat. Black barely noticed. Rats had been his constant companions for two years now, as had lice and the stench of rotting corpses. It was a testament to the army diet that this latrine could succeed in wrinkling his nose.

There was a shriek and a loud bang. Soil pattered down from the ceiling of the dugout. A second shriek and bang followed a second later.

"Fucking hell, don't start an artillery bombardment now, you filthy German buggers," Black grumbled.

A third shell hit not far off. A moment later a white shape hopped into the dugout.

Black stared. A rabbit. A fucking rabbit.

The rabbit stood at the entrance to the dugout, shivering all over, its ears twitching as another shell hit. It didn't appear to have seen Black.

When was the last time I saw a rabbit? Look at it, the poor thing's terrified.

Black eased up his pants and buttoned them. As he did up his belt the buckle made a slight clink.

The rabbit whipped around, spotted Black, and bolted out of the dugout.

"Wait!"

Another bang of an artillery shell brought the rabbit rushing right back in again.

"Careful, little chap. This is no place for you."

Black bent down and slowly reached out his hands. The rabbit seemed petrified with fear, pink eyes wide, white fur trembling. No more shells came down. Black almost wished for one. It would keep the rabbit in the latrine and make it easier to catch.

Black lunged forward. Soft fur brushed his hands and was gone. The rabbit flew outside.

"Come back!"

Black leapt out of the latrine and saw the rabbit loping down the communication trench, heading away from the firing line. No one else was about. He ran after it. The rabbit turned and scrabbled up the side of the trench and over the top.

"Damn it!"

Black poked his head over and saw the rabbit standing out on open ground. Against the mud it looked the purest white, like a thing from another world. For a moment he stood and looked at it with something akin to awe.

When Black was seven, a new family moved in next door. They built a hutch in their back garden and filled it with rabbits. The neighbors let him hop over the fence and play with them. He remembered how soft their fur was, how warm they were.

And he remembered the first time he saw the neighbors cut one of their heads off, strip the pelt, and throw the rabbit in a pot for dinner. He'd cried all night and never went next door again.

"Come back, you'll get shot out there," Black whispered.

Black glanced around. No one was looking. The shelling had stopped, just a bit of the usual morning hate sent over by Fritz.

Without really thinking about it, Black clambered over the lip of the trench. The ground was a little higher in the direction of the German trench so he should be OK as long as he kept low.

The rabbit loped a few yards further away.

"Come back," Black whispered.

Suddenly he realized what a stupid thing he was doing. What the hell was he out here for anyway?

The rabbit watched him with wary eyes. Black realized he'd never catch him this way. He had to stalk it, like he was stalking Germans during a raid.

He wormed his way to the left, away from the rabbit. There was a low mound which he might be able to get around and take the little chap by surprise.

Black winced as he pricked himself on some old wire half buried in the mud. He passed a discarded canteen, a battered helmet, and a shred of clothing that smelled like it contained the remains of its owner. He crawled in a half circle, coming around the mound. Yes, it looked like he'd be able to surprise Tommy.

Tommy? Sure, why not call him Tommy? Good old Tommy Atkins. That was what everyone called British soldiers, and he'd be the official mascot of the regiment. What better name than Tommy?

A loud crack of a Lee-Enfield rifle. Earth spat up inched from his face.

"I'm British, you silly bugger!" Black shouted.

"Oh, shit, mate," someone called from the support trench. "So you are. What are you doing out there?"

"Saving Tommy."

"Need a stretcher party?"

Black chuckled. "No, I think I can handle this."

I bloody well hope I can handle this.

The ground towards the German trench was more open at this spot. Black pressed himself against the mud and inched forward.

There he was—little Tommy sitting easy as you please next to a burst shell casing, whiskers twitching.

Black lunged.

"Got you!"

He didn't. Tommy leapt out of his grasp and disappeared into a shell crater a few feet ahead. Black leapt after him as a bullet zipped by. From the sound of it, it was a German Mauser this time.

Black tumbled into the shell crater and glimpsed a flash of white as Tommy jumped out, only to return a second later as a machine gun roared from the direction of the German trench. Tommy landed right into Black's arms.

"Shhhh," Black whispered as he stroked the little animal. "We've got ourselves some unwanted attention from Fritz, but I'll get you out. We'll fix you up a nice hutch in the dugout and feed you as sorts of goodies. You'll see."

The machine gun roared again, but Black knew the German crew was firing blind. Black was well out of sight inside the shell crater. He took a moment to look at his surroundings. The crater's bottom was filled with filthy water. On the slope opposite him, almost close enough to reach out and touch, lay a dead German, probably killed in that last attack three days ago. British and German bodies were mingled all over this sector. The man's chest was covered in blood, his face hidden by a gas mask. His Mauser lay nearby. With a sudden spike of panic, Black realized he had left his own rifle behind.

Black stroked his little friend until it stopped shivering. A feeling of calm came over him too.

"There you go, Tommy. Much better now, isn't it? Now we'll have to figure a way to get ourselves back, eh? We'll let Fritz over there get tired of shooting at nothing with his machine gun, and then we'll slip away, you and me."

A loud, hollow clonking rang out Black's chest clenched. The gas alarm. In the forward trench, not far from his dugout, someone was banging against an empty shell casing with a metal bar. The sentry had spotted a sickly yellow cloud of mustard gas heading across No Man's Land. A wave of German troops wouldn't be far behind.

Black grabbed his gas mask from its case and Tommy almost slipped from his grasp. He looked at the rabbit in panic. The little chap would die!

Wait, no, the German! Holding Tommy tight, Black scrambled over to the dead body. The German had a large empty pouch on his belt. It had probably contained a heap of grenades that he'd killed some of Black's friends with, the bastard. It was big enough to stuff Tommy into. If he tied him in, and put the German's gas mask over the opening, it might be enough to keep the little fellow alive.

Black stuffed Tommy into the bag.

"Don't be afraid," he whispered, giving it a final pat and drawing the string close. Tommy's pink nose poked out of the small opening.

"That's it, boy, I'll slip the mask just inside the opening, draw the string tight, and you'll be right as rain."

First Black put on his own mask, chuckling as he did. He hadn't turned into a complete lunatic. Once he checked he had a snug fit, he peeled off the mask from the dead German.

Black jerked backwards as the man groaned and turned his head. His face was young, with barely the wisp of stubble on his chin. Blue eyes fluttered open.

Black pushed the Mauser out of reach.

"Gas! Gas!" someone shouted from the trench. The hollow clanging of the gas alarm continued.

Black looked from the agonized face of the German down at Tommy's little pink nose poking out of the German's bag. He froze.

"*Mir helfen,*" the German groaned, reaching for Black with a trembling hand.

"Damn it!" Black shouted, batting the man's arm aside. He looked down at Tommy stuck in the German's bag. He touched the wet little nose sticking out. The German looked down too, confusion etched into his haggard face.

With a groan Black put the mask back on the German. He crawled out of the trench, not looking back. He was almost blind from blinking back tears as he crawled back to the communication trench. No German bullets sought him out. A noxious cloud the color of bile roiled forwards, blotting out the view. Black got into the trench, grabbed his rifle, and hurried to his post.

The next hour was a nightmare of jabbing bayonets, swinging rifles, screaming men. Yellow gas coiled through the trenches as Germans and British struggled for survival.

At last they pushed the assault back. The gas cleared and Black and his comrades busied themselves with clearing out the dead.

Black felt exhausted and spent. Several comrades had been killed, but he had thoughts only for one.

After a few hours he was put off duty and told to get some rest. Instead he went back to the crater. If that poor wounded German was alive he should bring him in. He had nothing to fear from the enemy trench this time. The Royal Artillery was giving them a heavy punishment. The German trenches plumed up with the spray of earth and body parts as shell after shell crumped into their position. No one over there would be looking out for a lone soldier crawling behind the lines. They were all too busy hunkering down in their own dugouts.

Black got to the shell crater and scrambled inside.

He stopped, and stared.

The German lay with his head uncovered, his face red and bloated, dried trickles of blood painting red lines from his mouth and nostrils. At his side lay his satchel. His gas mask was tied over the opening.

Stunned and unbelieving, Black crawled over to the satchel. He opened it up, pulling away the gas mask. The rabbit poked its head out.

"Hey little chap," Black said, cracking into a smile as he pet the rabbit. Then his face clouded over and he looked at the dead German. He laid a hand on the man's chest.

"Poor bugger."

He pulled the German's satchel off of him and put it around his own shoulder, tightening the drawstring so the rabbit couldn't escape. He closed the man's bloodshot eyes, then searched his pockets.

In his breast pocket, just above where a British bullet had wounded him so badly that he had spent his last days in this wretched shell hole,

Black found what he sought. A thin leather wallet held some German money, a letter, and a photograph.

It showed the soldier standing next to a young girl, too young to be his wife. A sister? Probably. They were standing in a back garden and holding two rabbits. The girl smiled at the camera, while the man wasn't even paying attention. Instead he had his nose buried in the soft fur of the rabbit in his arms.

"You weren't raising them for meat, were you?" Black whispered.

He opened up the letter. He couldn't read German, but the letter was written in a feminine hand, probably from this same sister. It was addressed to Fritz.

Black chuckled. "So some of you really are named Fritz, eh?"

The rabbit shifted within the satchel. Black realized that he should get back to the trench while he could. He put the photo and the letter back in the billfold and stuck it in his own pocket. He pulled the man's ID tag off his neck and put it with the billfold.

"We have an officer in our regiment who's right educated," he told the corpse. "Knows German as good as you once did. We'll find a way to write to your sis and tell her what you did."

Black turned away and crawled back to the trench.

As he got in, a sentry was waiting for him.

"Bloody hell, man, what you thinking?" the sentry gasped. "If one of the officers had spotted you, you'd be in for it!"

Black smiled. "I had to go save a friend."

He opened the satchel a little and the rabbit's head poked out.

"Oi, he's a cute little 'un," the sentry said, petting the rabbit with a grimy hand. "What's his name?"

Black didn't even have to think about it.

"Fritz. His name is Fritz."

SINKING

Private Billy Terraine was lagging behind. He squished through the knee-deep mud of the communication trench, sleepy and exhausted. The stretcher bearers ahead of him were beginning to disappear into the gathering gloom of another night on the Western Front.

One looked over his shoulder. "You all right?"

Terraine gave him a feeble wave with his good arm. The other hung in a sling, the shoulder swathed in bandages from where a German bullet had punched through the muscle.

"I'll catch you up," he said.

"Want me to stick with you?" Corporal Atkins asked. Atkins cradled his hand to his chest, a roll of bandages unable to hide his three missing fingers.

"Go on," Terraine told him.

They disappeared into the dusk as Terraine slogged along as best he could. All he wanted to do was sleep. One never got enough rest in the trenches, and the night before he'd gone into No Man's Land to string barbed wire, so he'd gotten less than usual. Then the Germans attacked and there had been fighting all day.

That bullet wound had almost come as a relief. It didn't hurt much and he wouldn't bleed out now that Dr. MacDonald had patched him up. But it meant two weeks in hospital and a month or so light duty helping some cook or quartermaster.

And that meant sleep. Blessed, blessed sleep. His eyes grew heavier at the thought. It was almost pitch dark now, and he stumbled along towards the rear by feel and memory. Every step through the quagmire was agony.

His leg hit something and he fell. He swore as he noticed a half-buried ammunition box. Imagine leaving that for anyone to trip over!

The temptation to sit nagged him, but he knew that would mean not arising until dawn, and he'd get it from the C.O.

Terraine leaned against the trench wall, legs encased in mud. He couldn't make it to the rear and he couldn't stay here.

Then he had another thought. He was far enough back that the low rise right behind the British forward trenches would be between him and the Germans. He could walk outside the trench and they wouldn't see him. Terraine and the lads had done that a few times after heavy rains flooded the communication trenches. None of them ever got hurt. You just had to be careful to hit the dirt anytime a shell came over.

He stepped on the box, hauled himself out, and lay panting on the trench lip. In the near darkness all he could see was mud on all sides, littered with broken rifles, discarded helmets, shell craters filled with stinking water, and a few kinked strands of barbed wire. A distant barrage flickered to the east, silhouetting a horizon devoid of any tree or structure. He staggered to his feet. The ground here was firmer. The mud only came up to the tops of his boots.

He made better time. Ah, it would be good to sleep. Another twenty minutes to the rear dressing station and he could sleep. Sleep through his evacuation, sleep through his convalescence, sleep, sleep, sleep.

Suddenly he was falling, plunging waist deep in cold water. Then his descent slowed but did not stop. By the time Terraine's muddled mind figured out what happened he was in up to his chest.

He'd fallen into a flooded shell crater, the water looking so much like mud that his tired eyes hadn't noticed.

Terraine resisted the urge to struggle. That was the worst thing to do. He eased his rifle off his good shoulder. The movement cost him another two inches.

He placed his rifle flat on the mud, below the surface of the water, and pressed his upper chest against it, trying to pull himself out and only managing to push the rifle out of reach into the sucking death below.

"Help!"

Terraine spread out his legs and good arm to make as big a surface as possible. That only slowed his sinking. His legs were stuck in mud so thick he could barely move them. His wounded arm flailed, trying to grasp something, anything. He reached with his good arm and his fingertips slid along the edge of the crater, taking off a clump of mud and widening the crater's edge so that it was out of reach.

"Help!"

A torch light winked on, the beam scanning the area. It found him and winked off.

"Coming, mate."

Terraine turned his head and felt the cold water rise over his collar to lap at his neck. He shivered but his heart leapt with hope as two shadowy figures rose out of the communication trench.

"Oi, you're in a bad way," one of them said as he extended his rifle with the butt towards Terraine. He grabbed it. That cost him another inch. He sputtered as water rose to his mouth.

"Pull!" his saviors said. Both men started hauling Terraine out of the crater. They groaned as they fought the mud's cold grip.

As the water got down to his chest a shrieking filled his ears. A German shell burst not ten yards away, blasting both his helpers off their feet. Terraine sank back down where he had come.

Another shell hit, and another. Through the flashes he could see both men lying in a tattered heap just beyond reach, the rifle flung out of sight. Each blast shook the water and mud encasing him and made him sink a little further.

Terraine slumped. The brief rescue attempt had taken the last of his energy. He was so tired. How could they let the men get so tired? Time to rest. Maybe he would stop sinking and someone would discover him in the morning. This mud made a comfortable bed. Chilly, but he was used to that. So tired.

Private Billy Terraine's eyes shut. By the time the water reached his neck he was asleep. It did not even wake him as it rose above his nose.

AFTER THE RAID

The bushwhackers had left. Helena Schmidt had lain weeping over her father's body in the front yard until the neighbors came. They took their time, eager to help but not wanting to run into the Confederate raiders who had shot her father. When they finally did arrive they made sympathetic noises. The men carried Lars Schmidt up the three steps of the porch, through the front door, and into the dining room where they laid him out on the table, wrapping him in a sheet until the undertaker could be called. The women had led Helena away.

That had been in the morning. Now it was night. The undertaker had come, declared the obvious, made it official by filling out a form, and took her father's body to the church until it could be buried. The men had all gone back to their shops and fields. The women Helena had to send away. Several offered to stay the night. Those who had rooms left vacant by their sons going off to war offered them to her. It took some time to make them understand that she wanted to stay in her own house and that she wanted to be alone. They left shaking their heads.

"Lars was such a quiet soul," they said. "Never spoke out against anybody. Why would the rebels want to kill him?"

Yes, why? Father never concerned himself about politics. While a Unionist and an abolitionist, he was not outspoken with his views. Being lame in one leg he wasn't part of Columbia's Union militia. He lived a life of quiet study, interacting with the public only through his photographic studio.

There had been six of them. They wore Union uniforms and flourished Union passes but Helena was suspicious from the start. They were too young, too cocky, too well-armed. They posed for a photograph and then gunned Father down.

As Helena sat benumbed in the study, her gaze wandered over her father's library—hundreds of books in half a dozen languages on all matters of the occult. Spiritism, theosophy, Gnostic cosmology, Hermeticism, geomancy.

Was this why they targeted him? The house stood close to the edge of town. It was dangerous for the bushwhackers to come here, and while they often targeted German civilians, they could have easily gone after those who lived in more isolated farms and vineyards. They hadn't wanted to kill a German; they had wanted to kill Lars Schmidt, and the only thing that distinguished him was his study of the occult. Yet few knew of his interests. It wasn't the sort of thing the staid civilians of Columbia would easily accept.

The bushwhackers hadn't touched her. "Cavaliers of the brush" these bandits called themselves, teenaged boys who read too many Arthurian romances and felt they were being chivalrous if they gunned an innocent man down in front of his daughter's eyes but didn't hurt the girl.

One of them had tried, though, when she called down the curse.

It was that wild-looking one, the one who had examined Father's library with knowing eyes. He knew that the words she'd used were a real curse and not some countrywoman's mumbo-jumbo. He'd leveled his pistol at her and got punched by one of the others.

"We don't make war on womenfolk!" the other one had said.

"Oh, but you have," she whispered as she sat in her father's study. "And I will make war on you."

What the wild-looking one didn't know was that she had no Power. Sometimes it is passed through the bloodline and sometimes it is not. Father had it, but his only child was a normal woman.

So the curse was nothing except words and spite. All it could do was make them nervous, not make them suffer. And they needed to suffer. She needed to make the curse real. The local militia captain had promised he would hunt them down but even if he was successful that wasn't enough. Death wasn't enough. Father had told her enough about death for her to know that it was nothing to fear.

Being raised by an occultist she knew many things that others only guessed at. Life lessons had a deeper meaning. When she was eight and Father caught her filching penny sweets from the local shop he didn't smack her bottom. Instead he sat her down and explained why that was wrong.

"All spirits have a frequency, child, like the tones on a musical scale. Those that are more pure have a higher frequency, and inhabit a bright place they share with all the greatest spirits of the ages. Those who steal, who kill, who live lives of greed and vituperation, those have low frequencies. They inhabit a dark place trapped with dirty spirits of their own kind."

"Is Mother in the bright place?" she had asked. Mother had died the year before.

"Yes, child," Father replied with a smile. "When I speak with her she tells me the most amazing things. We must live purely, so that when we pass from this world to the next we will be with her forever."

Helena had walked back to the store alone and tearfully confessed to the shopkeeper, returning the candy and doing chores to pay for those she'd already eaten.

Now Helena sat alone in Father's study. He and Mother were together in that place. Of that she was sure. He had always been a good man, a pure man. Honest and kind.

So why kill him? That's the question that burned in her mind. Did he know something the rebels wanted to hide?

Helena sat alone for a long time, her thoughts numb and her eyes unfocused.

She felt him before she saw him. One moment she was alone and the next she knew he was there.

She looked up. Something was materializing in the corner of the room.

Helena wasn't afraid. It was Father, so why should she be?

The faint outline of the portly man whom she had admired and loved all her life grew clearer. When he spoke his lips didn't move and he made no sound anyone but she could have heard.

Don't cry, Helena.

Helena tried not to.

"Are...are you with Mother? Are you in the bright place?" she managed to ask.

She slipped back to what she had called it as a child. She knew the occult terms for it—the Aetherial Plane, Goloka, Jannah, and many others—but seeing Father reduced to a shade made her feel like when she was seven years old and Mother died.

It's more beautiful than I ever imagined.

"What do I do now?"

Live well, as I taught you. And when your time comes you will join us.

"Those boys, those bushwhackers. They need to be punished! You never hurt anyone, why should they kill you?"

Her father shook his head.

They killed me because I chose a different path than they did. One of them comports with foul spirits and those spirits wanted me removed. They will be punished in the end.

"No, they need to be punished now! Not just death, not just going to the dark place. They need worse."

Have you forgotten all my lessons? That is not my way and it shouldn't be yours either.

"You have Power. You could come back and put them in a far lower place."

Again Father shook his head.

No. I would sink closer to their level. I would no longer be with your mother. And even if it were not for that I wouldn't do such a thing. Goodness is its own reward, even though goodness gives more rewards than its own nature.

Helena felt rage rise up in her, the same rage she'd felt when Father toppled to the ground with a bullet in his chest and she'd spat the curse at his murderers.

"Hunt them! Drag them down!"

No. I will go now and come back when you are calmer. I love you.

"Wait, don't go! I'm sorry. Stay a little longer," she pleaded.

But he was already fading.

Helena sat there fuming, her grief cut with anger. Father had always been too soft, too forgiving. When they'd seen Archibald Keyes whipping his slave by the side of the road, Helena had wanted to intervene, but Father had just snapped the reins to their buggy horse and sped past. "He'll suffer enough in the Afterlife, child."

It had been the same when the Sisters of the Union had invited her to join in their fundraising efforts back in '61 and Father had forbidden it. "We want no part in this war, child. Those who take up arms against their brothers pay for it in the Afterlife."

The Afterlife, the Afterlife, all he ever talked about was the spirit world. But she lived in this world, alone in a hostile country with no relations on this side of the Atlantic.

Father had said not to get involved in the war. Now the war had killed him and he was still saying not to get involved. Well, she was going to get involved, and in a more effective way than the Sisters of the Union with their bake sales and knitting bees.

But how? She couldn't don Union blue and go fight like the men did, and she didn't have the Power to make that curse on the bushwhackers effective.

Unless…

She walked out of her father's study and down a narrow corridor. One door opened into the photographic studio, where those evil boys had preened and posed for a tintype before gunning her father down. Opposite was the darkroom. The sharp smell of chemicals stung her nostrils. She blinked away tears. That smell always reminded her of Father.

At the end of the corridor hung a curtain of heavy black silk. She parted it and entered a small, windowless room. Striking a match, she lit the red candle that sat on a small gilt table next to the doorway.

This was her father's secret study, the one visitors didn't get to see.

The room was barely ten feet to a side, with paneled oak walls and a smooth floor of slate. Drawn in chalk in the center of the floor was a large pentagram surrounded by magical sigils. Facing it was a simple triangle. It was here that Father spoke to the various denizens of the spirit world—the dead and those things that had never lived. He would stand inside the pentagram for protection and would make the creatures appear in the triangle. Despite the popular fairy tales, he would not summon demons to go wreak havoc on the world. There were those who did such things, but Father steered clear of them.

"Their spirits are even lower than the unclean things they call from the Beyond," he would say.

Instead he summoned the shades of great men and women from bygone ages, and ethereal beings that had no name in any human language. He would stand there protected by his pentagram—for the wall between this world and the next had to be kept firm even if the beings he spoke with were beneficent—and the spirit would appear trapped in the triangle. For long hours through the night he would speak to them and learn the secrets of the universe.

Helena looked longingly at the chalk designs. If only she had the Power she could summon some fell being to strike down those boys, and to hell with the consequences. She had the knowledge. She had read many of Father's books and listened attentively when he spoke of his rituals, but without the Power it would be like a man struck blind trying to paint a sunset he remembered from childhood.

She turned to a low shelf standing to one side, stuffed with a few books and various items Father used in his rituals—a little gold bell, a flute made from the bone of a giant lizard that had lived in a bygone age, an astrolabe that measured the angles of stars that no uninitiated eye could see, and an ancient brass bowl.

This last item caught her attention. It was the pride of Father's collection, a relic of ancient Chaldea. Father had instructed her in its use. Unlike everything else, this required no Power or even knowledge to use. She picked it up lovingly and examined the strange script that ran in a spiral around the inside of the bowl.

She set it down and filled it with water from a crystal decanter. Bringing the candle closer, she peered into the water.

For a moment nothing happened. Then the water clouded as if she had mixed it with milk. The writing on the interior of the bowl wavered and faded from view. The surface of the liquid grew still and flat as a mirror and began to emit a pale light. Two figures materialized into view on its surface—her parents.

Helena smiled and they smiled back. Grief tugged at her again, mingled with relief to see them finally together again after being separated by the Veil for fifteen years.

She had looked through this bowl many times since Mother's death. Strange to think how she had grown from a girl to a young woman and Mother had remained ageless. Now Father would be the same way. They would watch as she grew older, become a mother perhaps, and grow into an old woman, while they remained beyond Time.

Helena smiled again and pointed to her father. She held up his pocket watch, pointed at it and then at him.

"Next time I wish to see you alone," she said, enunciating the words. The device could not transmit sound, but hopefully Father would understand her gestures and read her lips. He nodded.

For a moment parents and daughter stared at each other through the Veil, and then the image clouded over. The water cleared to as it was before.

Helena sighed. She poured the water back in the decanter and set to work. She had much to do. Time was of the essence, for if Father decided to materialize again before she reached him through the bowl, all would be lost.

Little did he know that his upbringing gave her all the knowledge she needed to defy his wishes.

While Father's passion had been the Hidden World, he had provided for his family well in the material one. He had built up a thriving photography business. He was one of the first men to open a daguerreotype studio in St. Louis back in the 1850s. When cheaper and easier tintypes were introduced late in the decade, competition became fierce in the city. He had sold the business, upped stakes, and moved to the outskirts of Columbia.

Once again he was among the first. Father proved an excellent technician and his photographs always gave satisfaction. Helena had a talent for painting the photographs, adding rosy cheeks to the babies or coloring in a man's favorite hat.

Helena had learned all aspects of the business. While the public wouldn't accept the idea of a woman taking their likeness, she often did the developing in the back room and arranged the lighting in the studio, giving the subjects just the right light at just the right angle.

It was this last skill that she needed now. She bustled around the house, collecting mirrors, ropes, and lamps.

Within an hour she had finished. Father's secret studio looked much different now. The bowl stood at the center of the summoning triangle. Above it hung two mirrors suspended by ropes from a hook she had hammered into the ceiling. One mirror hung parallel to the floor, reflecting the triangle and the bowl's interior. One was set behind the bowl and at an angle, so that it reflected the pentagram and the black crepe she had hung behind it. Lines of writing limned in fresh white paint ran down two edges of the crepe, with a space in between where Helena could stand.

With trembling hands Helena bent under the mirror and poured the contents of the decanter into the bowl. She rushed over to the pentagram and stood in the center.

From her vantage point the angled mirror behind the bowl showed her the interior of the bowl. She nodded in satisfaction. She had set it perfectly.

She stood, nervous, waiting.

The water clouded over. Father's face appeared. He smiled as he saw her reflection, thinking that he was looking directly at his daughter's face.

Then he looked around with a growing expression of horror.

One mirror reflected the bowl in which he had appeared, and the triangle around it. Father's head jerked to one side, and Helena knew he was looking at the other mirror's reflection.

It showed Helena standing in the middle of the pentagram. To either side he read his daughter's terrible command, her terrible mistake.

I LACK THE POWER TO SUMMON A DEMON TO DO THIS DEED, SO I SUMMON YOU. BY THE POWER OF THE PENTAGRAM AND TRIANGLE I COMMAND YOU. TAKE VENGEANCE ON THOSE WHO STRUCK YOU DOWN. CAST THEM TO THE LOWEST DARKNESS. YOU ARE BOUND BY THE MAGICAL SIGILS YOU YOURSELF DREW. YOU ARE UNDER COMPULSION. THE STAIN IS ON ME, NOT YOU. I AM SORRY FATHER.

Lars Schmidt's face contorted in despair. His image smeared, his wailing mouth stretching out in a silent scream.

And then he was gone.

Helena collapsed. The summoning had worked. Father would have to do the right thing now, and being forced into it he would not lose his place in the Light.

Helena, on the other hand, had stained her soul forever.

She wept for the second time that day, knowing that now death really was goodbye.

DANNEVIRKE

"Close that lantern!" the captain hissed. "The Prussians will see."

Jensen adjusted the wick, settled down on the frost-covered slope, and placed the lantern beside him. Open on only one side, it cast a feeble yellow glow onto him. The little pool of light seemed almost absorbed by the endless blackness surrounding us. He pulled a letter out of his gray overcoat and carefully opened it.

"Hey Jensen," I said. "The captain gave you an order."

"The rampart is high enough," Jensen replied, scanning the letter, "The Prussians won't see."

The captain scowled but said nothing. I shook my head. So this is what the Danish army had come to?

I grabbed my musket and scrambled up the slope, the frozen earth prickling my hands through my thin gloves. Despite being a thousand years old, the Dannevirke still stood high and steep, a thick berm cutting Jutland off from Germany. The earthwork had kept out the Germans in the days of King Harold Bluetooth, and our officers hoped it would keep them out again. My labored breath came in great white plumes as I hauled myself to the top.

We had recently dug a redoubt on the summit. Olaf and Anders crouched behind it, peering into the night.

"Any movement?" I whispered.

"Nothing," Olaf replied. His eyes shone under the brim of his cap as he scanned the night.

I looked out over the plain. The moon was near full, but a thin layer of cloud diffused its light to a pale, uniform glow, as if the sky had been wrapped in a winding sheet.

Patches of snow shone in the dim light. A few hundred yards south across the Schleswig plain the dark lines of the Prussian trenches cut through the white. They had arrived a few days before to find us holding the Dannevirke, the old Viking ramparts that had protected

Denmark from their kind all those years ago. The Prussians had dug trenches in the frozen earth and had set up their cannons. During the day they poured fire on us with artillery and repeating rifles. At night they kept quiet, waiting.

No light shone from their trenches. They were professional soldiers, not a bunch of fishermen and farmers called up from the parish militias like us.

A low rumble made me look to my left. Brief flashes silhouetted distant rooftops and church spires. The Prussians were bombarding Mysunde again. I listened for our batteries—honest Danish cannon sound different than those Krupp-made butcher machines—but heard none. There hadn't been return fire from Mysunde for more than a day now. Had the Prussians knocked out all our batteries, or had we run out of powder again?

Between our position and Mysunde I could see the Dannevirke as a long, dark shadow. On our side, at scattered intervals, shone a few lonely lights of other Danes trying to keep out the night, reminding me how stretched out our army was. Twenty men at our position, then a good two hundred paces before I could see any more of our troops. But the Prussian trenches, I knew, hid a solid line of soldiers just waiting for the right moment to overwhelm our positions and ravage our villages and farms.

I looked at the sky, hoping to see a break in the cloud. The thought of doing the ritual without any light made it more frightening somehow. I scrambled back down to the others huddled in the cold below.

"Are they back yet?" I asked as I joined them.

"No, they're still out there dowsing," the sergeant said.

"But Jensen's started the bombardment again," Hans added, grinning.

Some of the men laughed.

"That's not funny, those are Danes in that town," I snapped. Hans was from Copenhagen and laughed at everything, like city boys do.

The sergeant turned to Jensen.

"You better not let the higher ups see you with that light on."

The captain nodded in agreement.

Jensen shrugged and kept on reading.

"What's so important about that letter anyway?" I asked.

"It's from my cousin in America," Jensen replied.

"You've read that letter five times today!" Hans laughed.

"So what?" Jensen scowled at him. "I want to read it again."

"What does it say?" I asked.

"He joined the American army," Jensen replied.

"The North or the South?" I asked.

"The North," Jensen said. "He lives in Wisconsin. Wisconsin is in the North."

"Why is he fighting for the Negro?" I asked, irritated. "He should be here, fighting for Denmark."

"Why not?" Jensen replied. "In America they pay their soldiers with gold dollars. What do we get?"

"We get to defend our homes," the captain growled.

"And fight the Prussians," Sven added. "The Prussians are a Godless lot. Most aren't even Lutheran; they're Catholic. How can you trust a Catholic?"

"Well, he gets to fight down in Virginia. They don't have winter there. We're stuck out here in the middle of the night in February. I'd rather be in Virginia," Jensen said.

"He should be here with us, not fighting to free the Negroes," I insisted.

"I've never even seen a Negro," the sergeant said.

"I saw one once in Copenhagen," Hans said.

"Your cousin should be here," I said.

"Some of the Northern soldiers are getting breechloaders just like the Prussians have," Jensen said.

"I'd take a good Danish musket over some Prussian breechloader any day," I said.

"The Prussians can reload and fire four times for every shot we fire," the captain said. He had been to the Academy and knew these things.

"Well, don't we have more men?" Sven asked. "We don't need to do the ritual if we have more men."

The captain laughed bitterly.

"Have you looked over the Dannevirke lately?" he asked. "General de Meza says the Prussians outnumber us two to one."

"Who cares what General de Meza thinks?" Porsby asked. Porsby was a fisherman from Als, and he resented being so far from home. "He's never come out here to inspect our lines. How would he know anything?"

"You better not let the higher ups hear you!" the sergeant warned.

"What higher ups?" Porsby asked. "They're all in the town, warm in their beds."

Hans stuck his thumb in the direction of Mysunde.

"You mean that town?" Hans asked. A distant explosion emphasized his point.

Everyone laughed.

"They're beds are warm alright!" Porsby chuckled.

Porsby took out his pipe and lit it with a match. The stem disappeared under his heavy moustache and the coal glowed red as he sucked on the smoke.

"More light!" cried the captain, exasperated.

"How else am I going to keep warm?" Porsby asked.

I looked up at the sky. Still no moon.

"When are they coming back?" I asked.

"Wait. It will take time to find," the captain said.

Sven shook his head. He unbuttoned the top of his overcoat, reached under his scarf, and pulled out a cross on a chain. The silver caught the light of Jensen's lantern. Sven shivered and buttoned up his coat again.

"Do you want to sing a psalm?" Carl asked him. "My brother is a minister. He taught me all of them."

"Alright," Sven said.

"There will be no psalm singing," the captain stated, his voice authoritative for once. "It might affect the ritual."

Sven looked hurt. He gazed at the cross for a long time before putting back it under his scarf.

"This is wrong," he said. "No good will come of this."

"Just one, captain?" Carl asked.

"No."

"What will my brother say?" Carl sighed.

"I'm going to sing anyway. You can't tell us not to sing psalms!" Sven said, suddenly angry.

"No singing," The captain said.

"The Lord is my light and my salvation—whom shall I fear? The Lord is the stronghold of my life—of whom shall I be afraid?"

"No singing!"

"When evil men advance against me to devour my flesh, when my enemies and my foes attack me, they will stumble and fall," Sven continued. Carl joined him, singing in a soft voice.

"QUIET!" the captain bellowed.

"Though an army besiege me, my heart will not fear, though war break out against me even th..."

"Shut up," a woman's voice snapped.

Sven and Carl broke off midword. Even in the dim light I could see them turn pale. A few feet away stood the old peasant couple. They had returned.

My heart turned to ice. The old man and woman wore only thin jackets over tattered clothing, but they didn't seem to notice the chill of the night. They stood tall and rigid as they looked down on us, the diffuse moonlight giving their pale skin a waxy, dead look. The man, who never spoke, looked so thin his cheek bones jutted out as if they would cut through his taut, papery skin. He had a hot gleam in his eye that I could not bear to look upon. The woman held a rod of oak in one hand, split at the end to make a "Y."

"We have found them," she announced.

I wrapped my overcoat closer about me and shivered. The couple had come to us two days before. At first we thought they lived on one of the nearby farms, but the locals told us they had never seen them before. The couple claimed they had a way to defeat the Prussians, and the solution they proposed was so outlandish, so unbelievable, no one dared laugh. One look at them and we knew they meant what they said. They were either mad or very, very dangerous. Despite protests from some of the men, the captain agreed, saying we needed every chance. But now, now that they stood in front of us ready to start the ritual, my heart quailed and I doubted I could go through with it. Looking at the others, I could see they felt the same.

Carl spoke first.

"Captain," his voice broken. "Maybe there's some other way."

"What other way?"

"Maybe we could beat the Prussians in battle."

"The Prussians don't lose battles."

Carl's head drooped. It was true. The Prussians didn't lose battles.

"What will my brother say?" he whispered.

"Your brother will never believe it happened," the captain said, "and he will be proud of you for defeating the Prussians."

We sat silent for a time, the only sound the distant rumble of cannon fire towards the town. A red glow illumined its skyline. Something was burning over there.

"We must go," the old woman said, her face turned crimson by the distant flames. "The ritual must be completed before sunrise."

Reluctantly we got to our feet. The captain drew his sword and arranged us in ranks. He sent a few up to the top of the Dannevirke to help Olaf and Anders keep watch.

"Sergeant!" he barked.

"Yes, sir!" the sergeant replied. The sergeant was the only one who ever called the captain "sir." Not that he took him any more seriously than the rest of us, but the sergeant was a career man and liked things proper.

"Go get the prisoner."

"Yes, sir," the sergeant left.

I approached the captain.

"Do you think it's wise to bring Carl and Sven along?" I whispered. "They've been against this from the start. They might cause trouble."

"I'd rather have them where I can watch them." he whispered back. "If we leave them they might tell someone."

A few moments later the sergeant returned with the prisoner, a Prussian scout we had caught the previous evening. The captain had interrogated him in both Danish and German, but the scout never uttered a word. We kept him anyway, not telling the higher officers. We had a better use for him than interrogation.

We all stood around, silent. For the first time that night the Prussians had ceased to matter. I realized I had been worrying about the enemy so that I didn't have to think about what we meant to do.

"Who will make the sacrifice?" the old man asked, speaking for the first time. His voice sounded hollow and very distant.

Everyone looked at the captain. He fidgeted, shifting from foot to foot.

"Well," he said at last, "I guess it should be me."

"A warrior needs to do it," the old woman said, eying him. "Are you a warrior?"

The captain stood a little straighter and grasped the holster of his pistol.

"Madam, I trained at the Royal Military Academy in Copenhagen. General de Meza himself gave me a service medal."

The old woman said nothing.

Hans and Porsby stood on either side of the Prussian, guarding him. He looked tired and depressed, but not afraid. Someone gave him a cigarette and he stood there, slouched, blowing resentful clouds of smoke around him. The pale gray puffs of tobacco mingled with the white vapor of our breath. I found it hard to look at him, and stole guilty glances from the corner of my eye.

"Let's go," the sergeant said.

"This is wrong," Sven said. "I want no part of it."

"Shut up and march," the sergeant ordered. The only sound was the crackle of frosted grass underfoot. I wrapped my scarf around my mouth and nose to keep out the increasing chill and watched the Prussian as we walked. I told myself I was making sure he didn't run, but as I look back on it now I realize I wished he would have.

The old couple led us to the spot they had found. It stood a few hundred yards away, in a pasture behind a hedge. The Dannevirke appeared as a low, dark mass against the clearing sky. Stars burned still and cold above us. A gibbous moon shone through thinning clouds.

On the ground we saw a rectangular area three or four paces by about eight paces. They had marked it with the stick, scraping a deep furrow into the frozen ground. I wondered how they could be so strong as to do that.

Hans, Porsby, and the sergeant produced shovels and began to dig into the topsoil. The couple stood to either side of the rectangle, chanting in guttural tones. The men's grunts as they labored against the hard soil mixed with the chanting.

The Prussian finished his cigarette and dropped the butt end on the ground, its bright red tip falling like a meteor, making an almost inaudible hiss as it hit the frost, melted it, and was in turn extinguished.

"This isn't right," Sven said.

"Quiet," the sergeant ordered, wiping his brow as he shoveled frozen dirt.

When the three men finished, the old couple, still chanting, began to scrape symbols onto the bare earth. Their chanting rose, gaining strength and I stood fascinated as I watched their work.

My town, Ravensbjerg, has a good harbor. It lies on the northern tip of Jutland, facing the grey waters of the North Sea. In old times, they say, the Vikings used it as a base for their raids on England and France. A short walk from the harbor is a spit of land that reaches into the sea like a finger. At its very tip stands a rune stone. No one in Ravensbjerg could read what is written on it, but I loved to go out there and trace the strange signs with my finger, wondering about the proud, brave Danes who had carved them. I recognized some of the signs the strange pair drew in the dirt, and realized with a sudden joy that the language these two were chanting was Old Norse. Here, at this ancient defensive line against German barbarism, there still lived people who knew the old ways. Confidence surged in me, and I knew what we were doing was right.

The couple finished and stood to either side of the rectangle.

"It is time," the woman said.

Hans pushed the Prussian hard in the back so he stumbled forward into the rectangle. He staggered for a moment, caught his balance, and tried to walk back. We levelled our muskets. A dozen bayonets gleamed in the moonlight.

"Run him through with your sword," the woman told the captain.

We all looked at the captain. He had turned pale, and despite the cold his face was beaded with sweat that trickled down to soak his scarf.

"I...uh," he fumbled for his pistol, and only just managed to pull it from the holster without dropping it.

"I'll...I'll shoot him," he stammered.

"Use your sword," the woman repeated.

"What difference does it make?" he asked, his voice shrill. "I'll use the pistol."

"The sacrifice should be performed with a blade, like in the old times," the old man said.

The captain trembled, his pistol wavering like a fish thrown ashore.

"I'll shoot him," he said.

"Captain, I beg of you, don't do this," Sven said.

"This is wrong," Carl said.

"You should use the blade," the old man repeated.

"Yeah, stick him!" Hans called out.

The Prussian's eyes flicked back and forth as he tried to understand what was being said. He had curled in on himself and looked very small, as if he were trying to disappear.

"Stick him. Why don't you stick him?" Hans persisted.

"He's afraid to get his hands bloody," Porsby said.

"What's the matter, captain? Afraid to see his guts spill out?" Hans taunted.

"Shut up!" the captain shouted. "Do you want to stick him?"

Hans didn't answer.

"I'll shoot him," the captain declared. "That's good enough."

"Captain, please no," Sven said.

With a visible effort the Captain controlled his trembling hand and pointed the revolver at the Prussian. The Prussian glanced this way and that, searching for an escape that wasn't there. He blinked once, then seemed to become very awake. He looked straight at the captain and stood tall and proud, chest pushed out.

Silence, just for a moment.

Then a sharp report and a flash in the night.

The Prussian jerked a little, took a step back and fell, twisting, to the ground. He coughed—a wet, sickening sound—and let out a little moan as blood ran from his chest. That was all.

"No!" Sven cried. He darted towards the Prussian. In a flash the old man grabbed him and picked him off his feet. I heard a sickening snap as he pushed Sven's head back. The old man tossed his body on the ground.

No one moved. The captain groaned in anguish, but his expression showed resignation. I realized he knew something like this would happen the moment he ordered Sven and Carl to come to the ritual with us. Carl stood very still, as if hoping the old couple might not notice him.

They didn't touch him, because a moment later all eyes turned back to the ritual area.

The two started chanting again. I watched, with equal parts fascination and horror, as the Prussian's blood spread out in a dark puddle, collecting in the sigils carved into the soil while glimmering with a brighter light than could be explained by the moon. The pool spread, impossibly quickly, until it filled the cleared area of the rectangle. A chill gust lifted the steam towards the cold stars above. The couple's chanting rose in intonation until they were wailing—a pleading, dissonant dirge I am grateful I could not understand.

All races have secrets. All peoples have one thing that makes them what they are, although sometimes they would be more comfortable denying it. For the Prussians, it is their natural cunning at fashioning machines of war. For us Danes, it is the old ways that I now know never died. It is the Viking magic beneath the thin, ardent veneer of Sven and Carl's Christianity, like the worms of a mulch pit beneath the green grass that covers it.

In the next moment, I knew that in the veins of the peaceful fisherfolk of Ravensbjerg and the stolid farmers of Jutland ran the pagan blood of Vikings, and that blood could never be drained. I have always been proud of my heritage, proud of my history, but in the next moment I became afraid of it too, afraid of what I knew to be in my bones, my soul. For in that next moment, under the dim light of Jensen's lantern, what little innocence I had left was torn away.

The blood made a shallow pool. It spread too quickly to be natural, and stayed too long on the surface. But then it suddenly sank into the earth, leaving only foul-smelling wisps of steam. From the damp soil came a faint throbbing. The ground beneath our feet vibrated, resonating with an unearthly beat as if from the drummer of some spectral legion.

The earth heaved. A ragged, bloody arm tore out through the soil and grasped onto a clod of earth. A dark figure pushed out of the ground. Another rose next to it, and another. Someone screamed. A musket went off. I stood frozen as I watched my ancestors rise from the grave.

For they were Vikings. No Dane could mistake the fur robes and the muscular bodies, or the broad axes and keen swords that the figures held. Their tattered flesh glistened with blood, the Prussian's blood, and their bodies seemed to soak it up and fill out, becoming whole once again.

Soon they stood before us, a score of ancient warriors brought back to life by a heathen ritual. Awestruck, I gazed at the Vikings before me, and despite my fear and revulsion, despite my guilt over Sven's death, I could not help but feel proud to see the strong forebears of my race.

****

The next day dawned cold and grey and it looked as if it would snow. We huddled close together, as much for security as warmth. The Vikings didn't seem to notice the cold. They stood stiff and erect atop the Dannevirke, their frost-covered faces turned mutely towards the Prussian lines.

A biting wind moaned out of the north, mixing with the mad babbling of Carl. His mind had snapped and we had left him behind the Dannevirke. His words were mostly nonsense, punctuated by shrill laughter and floods of tears. At times he seemed to be speaking to someone, asking forgiveness.

As it grew light I looked up and down our defenses. Small knots of men stood behind redoubts every few hundred paces. The closest was too far away to see that the warriors who had joined us were not living men, and the captain and sergeant made sure that the other units stayed in their positions, away from us.

Out in the Prussian trenches we could see movement. The early sun gleamed on steel cannon and sharp bayonets.

"What if the Prussians attack another section of the Dannevirke?" the captain asked the old woman.

"They will attack here," she replied. "That is why your unit was chosen to help with the ritual."

"It went alright, didn't it?" I asked. "I mean to say, the captain didn't use the sword, but the ritual worked. So everything's fine…right?"

"The ritual should have been performed according to the old rite," she replied.

I looked at the Vikings. Despite their rotted clothing and sickly pallor, pride shone in every fiber of their being. They stood straight, tall, in command of the land that they had guarded before.

"Magnificent, aren't they?" I said. "We'll hand the Prussians such a defeat that they won't invade for another thousand years!"

"But…" the captain's voice trailed off, then he seemed to gather confidence. "There are so few of them, how will they defeat the Prussians?"

The old woman gave him a disdainful glare.

"You fool. They are the dead. Magic flows in their veins. Do you think bullets will do them any harm?"

The captain didn't reply.

"Look!" the sergeant cried.

The trenches directly in front of us came alive. A thick mass of Prussians streamed over the top and charged, a sea of blue uniforms flooding the frosty plain. There must have been hundreds of them, all within the small area in front of our position. There had been no preliminary bombardment, no bugles, nothing to warn us. One moment the lines lay quiet, expectant, the next moment the attack commenced. I could see more of their units drawing up behind their trenches. It was obvious the Prussians wanted to break our line right there and pour men into the gap.

"Fire!" the captain ordered.

I levelled my musket, aimed into the crowd, and pulled the trigger. The musket bucked in my hands and my eyes stung as a cloud of gun smoke hit them. I saw a Prussian fall. A few more fell, too few, as my comrades fired also. I reloaded, cursing the army as I fumbled with the powder and the shot, priming the pan and ramming the bullet home. The gun reloaded too slowly, too slowly to get more than one more shot off before that wave of men would be scaling our defenses. What a fool I had been to respect such an outdated weapon! Why hadn't our government invested in breechloaders? I could have shot four, maybe six Prussians before they made it to us.

I finally reloaded my gun and aimed, but before I could fire the old man gave out a guttural cry, and the Vikings, as one body, charged down the Dannevirke and into the onrushing horde. They ran in silence, weapons held at the ready. The Prussians, now at the base of the rampart, stopped in amazement at the sight of twenty men charging their hundreds. I could see them looking at each other in disbelief. Then they aimed their rifles and fired.

A mad whine of bullets filled the air. Each Viking got hit by a dozen or more. They jerked and lurched from the force of them, but kept charging.

A cheer rose up from our unit and carried down our line as others saw our ancestor's brave counterattack. From where the other units stood they must have thought it was us. None would have suspected, or believed if they had been told, that the original defenders of the Dannevirke fought for Denmark once more.

The Prussians fired again and again, reloading at a furious rate, but they could not stop that terrible charge.

The Vikings set upon them, swinging their axes and swords, and the Prussians fell like wheat at harvest time. Within moments they fled back to their trenches, screaming in terror. They had seen what our own army could never suspect. Their famous martial willpower was broken.

The Vikings stood in a little group, surrounded by heaps of dismembered bodies, the ground soaked in hot blood, the evaporated frost rising in a russet steam. They waved their weapons above their heads, mocking the Prussians cowering in their trenches. A strange, harsh song rose from their dead lips, a war chant unheard for a thousand years, and we joined in with the national anthem. My heart swelled with pride. We had done it! Denmark was safe!

A dull roar erupted from the Prussian lines. A cannonball ripped through the crowd of Vikings, shattering half a dozen and scattering their pieces across the plain. Another cannon fired, and another, with cruel, diabolical accuracy, and within moments our brave band of Vikings was nothing but a smoldering scatter of limbs and torsos.

As we watched in despair, they began to decompose at an unnatural rate, their flesh rotting away, baring bones that cracked and turned to dust. Soon all that remained were the dead Prussians, smoking craters, and a fine dust blown away with the first flakes of falling snow.

****

We retreat north through a howling blizzard. Wind tears at our overcoats and whips hail into our faces Men collapse by the side of the road, exhausted by our long retreat. Only a few of my unit are around me. Porsby has survived, and Hans too. The sergeant took a bullet through the chest and is carried, moaning, on a stretcher. Everyone else got killed in the attack, all but for the captain, who, when he saw the Vikings fall, put his pistol in his mouth and blew his brains out.

And the old peasant couple? They are gone. As the Prussians swarmed over the Dannevirke we lost track of them. I hope the Prussians cut them down, as they cut down so many of my fellow Danes, but I do not think so.

A long line of refugees follows the army. Men push carts filled with all their worldly belongings. Women hug shivering babes to their chests and stab us with accusing looks through red-rimmed eyes. We had sought to defend their lands, but now they have lost their homes and their farms.

We are no better. There is no rearguard action, no plans to regroup. Every man is running, staggering really, to the north. No goal in mind except home, no motivation but to get away from the Prussians.

Denmark is defeated. We summoned the spirit of our land and it failed us. Why did the spell not work? Was it as simple as the difference between a blade and a pistol? In the end, did we fail because we could not put our full faith in the ancient rite?

But perhaps we had been fools to believe it would work. We were defeated because the Prussians have more advanced weapons. The machines of the modern age can kill even the dead.

Prussia is the future, and we are the past. Through sheets of hail I gaze out over the flat fields and isolated farmhouses. This land is theirs now. Schleswig will become German, as the Prussians had always claimed it was. Our old kingdom will fade while their empire, built on industry and discipline, will grow.

About the Author

Sean McLachlan worked for ten years as an archaeologist in Israel, Cyprus, Bulgaria, and the United States before becoming a full-time writer. He is the author of numerous fiction and nonfiction books, which are listed on the following pages. When he's not writing, he enjoys hiking, reading, traveling, and, most of all, teaching his son about the world. He divides his time between Madrid, Oxford, and Cairo.

To find out more about Sean's work and travels, visit him at his blog[1], his website[2], and feel free to friend him on Goodreads[3] and Facebook[4].

You might also enjoy his newsletter[5], *Sean's Travels and Tales*, which comes out every one or two months. Each issue features a short story and/or a travel article, updates on future projects, and sometimes a coupon for a free or discounted book! You can subscribe using this link[6]. Your email will not be shared with anyone else.

---

1.   http://midlistwriter.blogspot.com

2.   https://www.seanmclachlan.net/

3.   http://www.goodreads.com/author/show/523273.Sean_McLachlan

4.   https://www.facebook.com/writersean

5.   http://eepurl.com/bJfiDn

6.   http://eepurl.com/bJfiDn

Fiction by Sean McLachlan

Trench Raiders (Trench Raiders Book One)

September 1914: The British Expeditionary Force has the Germans on the run, or so they think.

After a month of bitter fighting, the British are battered, exhausted, and down to half their strength, yet they've helped save Paris and are pushing towards Berlin. Then the retreating Germans decide to make a stand. Holding a steep slope beside the River Aisne, the entrenched Germans mow down the advancing British with machine gun fire. Soon the British dig in too, and it looks like the war might grind down into deadly stalemate.

Searching through No-Man's Land in the darkness, Private Timothy Crawford of the Oxfordshire and Buckinghamshire Light Infantry finds a chink in the German armor. But can this lowly private, who spends as much time in the battalion guardhouse as he does on the parade ground, convince his commanding officer to risk everything for a chance to break through?

Available in electronic and print editions!

Digging In (Trench Raiders Book Two)

October 1914: The British line is about to break.

After two months of hard fighting, the British Expeditionary Force is short of men, ammunition, and ideas. With their line stretched to the breaking point, aerial reconnaissance spots German reinforcements massing for the big push. As their trenches are hammered by a German artillery battery, the men of the Oxfordshire and Buckinghamshire Light Infantry come up with a desperate plan—a daring raid behind enemy lines to destroy the enemy guns and give the British a chance to stop the German army from breaking through.

Available in electronic and print editions!

No Man's Land (Trench Raiders Book Three)

No Man's Land—a hellscape of shell craters and dead bodies. Soldiers have fought over it, charged across it, and bled on it for a year of grueling war, but neither side has dominated it.

Until now.

An elite German raiding party is passing through No Man's Land every night, attacking the British trenches at will. The Oxfordshire and Buckinghamshire Light Infantry need to reassert control over their front lines.

So the exhausted men of Company E decide to set a trap, a nighttime ambush in the middle of No Man's Land, where any mistake can be fatal. But the few surviving veterans are leading recruits who have only been in the trenches for two weeks. Mistakes are inevitable.

Available in electronic and print editions!

Christmas Truce

Christmas 1914

In the cold, muddy trenches of the Western Front, there is a strange silence. As the members of a crack English trench raiding team enjoy their first day of peace in months, they call out holiday greetings to the men on the German line. Soon both sides are fraternizing in No Man's Land.

But when the English recognize some enemy raiders who only a few days before launched a deadly attack on their position, can they keep the peace through the Christmas truce?

Available in electronic and print editions!

Warpath into Sonora

Arizona 1846

Nantan, a young Apache warrior, is building a name for himself by leading raids against Mexican ranches to impress his war chief, and the chief's lovely daughter. But there is one thing he and all other Apaches fear—a ruthless band of Mexican scalp hunters who slaughter entire villages.

Nantan and his friends have sworn to fight back, but they are inexperienced, and led by a war chief driven mad with a thirst for revenge. Can they track their tribe's worst enemy into unknown territory and defeat them?

Available in electronic and print editions!

A Fine Likeness (House Divided Book One)

A Confederate guerrilla and a Union captain discover there's something more dangerous in the woods than each other.

Jimmy Rawlins is a teenage bushwhacker who leads his friends on ambushes of Union patrols. They join infamous guerrilla leader Bloody Bill Anderson on a raid through Missouri, but Jimmy questions his commitment to the cause when he discovers this madman plans to sacrifice a Union prisoner in a hellish ritual to raise the Confederate dead.

Richard Addison is an aging captain of a lackluster Union militia. Depressed over his son's death in battle, a glimpse of Jimmy changes his life. Jimmy and his son look so much alike that Addison becomes obsessed with saving him from Bloody Bill. Captain Addison must wreck his reputation to win this war within a war, while Jimmy must decide whether to betray the Confederacy to stop the evil arising in the woods of Missouri.

Available in print and electronic editions!

The River of Desperation (House Divided Book Two)

In the waning days of the Civil War, a secret conflict still rages...

Lieutenant Allen Addison of the *USS Essex* is looking forward to the South's defeat so he can build the life he's always wanted. Love and a promising business await him in St. Louis, but he is swept up in a primeval war between the forces of Order and Chaos, a struggle he doesn't understand and can barely believe in. Soon he is fighting to keep a grip on his sanity as he tries to save St. Louis from destruction.

The long-awaited sequel to *A Fine Likeness* continues the story of two opposing forces that threaten to tear the world apart.

Available in electronic and print editions!

Tangier Bank Heist: An Interzone Mystery

Right after the war, Tangier was the craziest town in North Africa. Everything was for sale and the price was cheap. The perverts came for the flesh. The addicts came for the drugs. A whole army of hustlers and grifters came for the loose laws and free flow of cash and contraband.

So why was I here? Because it was the only place that would have me. Besides, it was a great place to be a detective. You got cases like in no other place I'd ever been, and I'd been all over. Cases you couldn't believe ever happened. Like when I had to track down the guy who stole the bank.

No, he didn't rob the bank, he stole it.

Here's how it happened . . .

Available in electronic and print editions!

Three Passports to Trouble (Interzone Mystery Book 2)

Back in the days when Tangier was an International Zone, the city was full of refugees. People fleeing Stalin. People fleeing Franco. People fleeing the Nuremburg Trials. Tangier offered a safe haven from the chaos of Europe.

The International Council had to keep a delicate balance, tolerating everything from anti-capitalist agitators to Germans with murky pasts. It was the only way to keep the peace, and it worked.

Until an anarchist was found dead with a fascist dagger in his chest.

And I got stuck with the case just when I had to smuggle a couple of Party operatives out of town.

Available in electronic and print editions!

Flight to Fez (Interzone Mystery Book Three)

Only in Tangier could a literary event turn into a murder scene.

I'm "Shorty" MacAllister, private detective. I've investigated all sorts of crazy cases in this lawless town, tracking down con men and Nazi fugitives, anarchists and bank robbers, all the while running my own secret angle.

But I never thought that when I went to hear my friend Jane Bowles read her latest story I'd end with a murdered man in my lap, and an old war buddy getting pinned with the crime.

After that, things got a whole lot more complicated.

Available in electronic and print editions!

The Case of the Purloined Pyramid (The Masked Man of Cairo Book One)

An ancient mystery. A modern murder.

Sir Augustus Wall, a horribly mutilated veteran of the Great War, has left Europe behind to open an antiquities shop in Cairo. But Europe's troubles follow him as a priceless inscription is stolen and those who know its secrets start turning up dead. Teaming up with Egyptology expert Moustafa Ghani, and Faisal, an irritating street urchin he just can't shake, Sir Wall must unravel an ancient secret and face his own dark past.

Available in electronic and print editions!

The Case of the Shifting Sarcophagus (The Masked Man of Cairo Book Two)

An Old Kingdom coffin. A body from yesterday.

Sir Augustus Wall had seen a lot of death. From the fields of Flanders to the alleys of Cairo, he'd solved several murders and sent many men to their grave. But he's never had a body delivered to his antiquities shop encased in a 5,000 year-old coffin.

Soon he finds himself fighting a vicious street gang bent on causing national mayhem while his assistant, Moustafa Ghani, faces his own enemies in the form of colonial powers determined to ruin him. Throughout all this runs the street urchin Faisal. Ignored as usual, dismissed as usual, he has the most important fight of all.

Available in electronic and print editions!

The Case of the Golden Greeks (The Masked Man of Cairo Book Three)

They thought the case was solved.

When an eminent Egyptologist is murdered giving a lecture in front of a packed hall, Cairo's chief of police quickly rounds up those responsible.

Or at least some of them.

Sir Augustus Wall, antiquities dealer and amateur sleuth, knows there's more to the crime than it seems. With little to go on but an exotic murder weapon, a map of a desert oasis, and some gilded Greek mummies, he sets out across the Sahara with his assistant Moustafa Ghani and the street urchin Faisal, who is the only person to have seen the killer's face. They soon find themselves in the midst of international intrigue on Egypt's remote border with Libya.

Can they discover what mystery lies beneath Bahariya Oasis?

Available in electronic and print editions!

The Case of the Karnak Killer (The Masked Man of Cairo Book Four)

A scandal in America. A murder in Cairo.

Sir Augustus Wall, antiquities dealer and amateur sleuth, is hired to track down a blackmailer who threatens the reputation of an American millionaire. When blackmail turns to murder, he must travel up the Nile by steamboat to find the killer.

Joining him are Faisal, a street urchin who makes himself equally useful and troublesome; Heinrich Schäfer, a leading Egyptologist; and Jocelyn Montjoy, an adventurous woman who has captured his heart.

But complications set in before the hunt even begins. Unwelcome fellow passengers threaten to derail the investigation, and Augustus has fallen out with his right-hand man, Moustafa Ghani. Can a new team of investigators help him solve his most challenging case yet?

Available in electronic and print editions!

The Case of the Asphyxiated Alexandrian (The Masked Man of Cairo Book 5)

A mysterious murder. A lost pharaoh.

Sir Augustus Wall came to Egypt to escape his old life, but when a comrade from the trenches is found murdered in a Cairo hotel, Augustus realizes his past has finally caught up.

Now he must discover the reason for the baffling murder, leading him and his friends Moustafa and Faisal on a dangerous hunt for the most sought-after treasure in Egypt.

The long-awaited fifth book in the Masked Man of Cairo series sees the trio on their greatest adventure yet!

Available in electronic and print editions!

The Case of the Dastardly Djinn (A Masked Man of Cairo Prequel)

A homeless boy. A hunted girl.

Cairo, 1917. In a city plagued by poverty and war, ten-year-old Faisal begs and steals to survive, hiding at night from the things that prowl after dark. The nimblest and most clever of the street boys, he's terrified of the unseen spirits he's convinced haunt the ancient city.

But when he discovers a girl his age left homeless by a terrible tragedy, Faisal decides to do what no one ever did for him—help. With no shelter and facing the many dangers of Cairo's darkened streets, Faisal's loyalties are tested when together they uncover a criminal ring more sinister than his worst superstitions.

This prequel to the Masked Man of Cairo mystery adventure series will thrill new readers and long-time fans alike!

A portion of the proceeds from this book will go to help Egyptian street children.

Available in electronic and print editions!

A Winter Murder in Berlin (The Berlin Murders Book One)

The voyage of a lifetime turns into a nightmare.

When Katherine Schmidt sails for Europe in late 1929, she looks forward to a year of carefree travel thanks to an unexpected inheritance. But when a companion on her steamer is murdered and she becomes a suspect, she needs to find the real killer before the police close in. Now she must delve into Weimar Berlin's decadent nightlife and radical politics in order to clear her name.

Can an innocent young woman from Missouri outwit fascists, communists, and the denizens of Berlin's notorious shadow world?
Available in electronic and print editions!

Radio Hope (Toxic World Book One)
In a world shattered by war, pollution and disease...

A gunslinging mother longs to find a safe refuge for her son.

A frustrated revolutionary delivers water to villagers living on a toxic waste dump.

The assistant mayor of humanity's last city hopes he will never have to take command.

One thing gives them the promise of a better future—Radio Hope, a mysterious station that broadcasts vital information about surviving in a blighted world. But when a mad prophet and his army of fanatics march out of the wildlands on a crusade to purify the land with blood and fire, all three will find their lives intertwining, and changing forever.

Available in print and electronic editions!

Refugees from the Righteous Horde (Toxic World Book Two)
When you only have one shot, you better aim true.

In a ravaged world, civilization's last outpost is reeling after fighting off the fanatical warriors of the Righteous Horde. Sheriff Annette Cruz becomes New City's long arm of vengeance as she sets off across the wildlands to take out the cult's leader. All she has is a sniper's rifle with one bullet and a former cultist with his own agenda. Meanwhile, one of the cult's escaped slaves makes a discovery that could tear New City apart...

Refugees from the Righteous Horde continues the Toxic World series started in Radio Hope, an ongoing narrative of humanity's struggle to rebuild the world it ruined.

Available in electronic edition!

We Had Flags (Toxic World Book Three)

A law doesn't work if everyone breaks it.

For forty years, New City has been a bastion of order in a fallen world. One crucial law has maintained the peace: it is illegal to place responsibility for the collapse of civilization on any one group. Anyone found guilty of Blaming is branded and stripped of citizenship.

But when some unwelcome visitors arrive from across the sea, old wounds break open, and no one is safe from Blame.

Available in electronic edition!

Emergency Transmission (Toxic World Book Four)

Trust is the only thing that can save the world.

The problem is, everyone has their own agenda.

When an offshore platform starts emitting toxic fumes that threaten to destroy the last outposts of civilization, the residents of New City have to team up with a foreign freighter to fix it. But a lingering mistrust remains, and neither side has the resources to stop the leak.

That is, until help comes from the least reliable source.

Can old enemies finally set aside their differences for the greater good?

Available in electronic edition!

Tales from the Toxic World

A scavenger with a wondrous artifact from the Old Times sets out to avenge his past ...

The sheriff of a post-apocalyptic shantytown investigates a baffling murder ...

Two fishermen in a toxic sea make a startling discovery ...

A peddler has to compromise his faith to help others and not end up dead ...

Here are nine stories from a grim future that's all too possible. The world has been destroyed by war, pollution, and environmental degradation. Now only a few lonely outposts struggle to keep the light of civilization lit amid vast toxic wasteland filled with human predators.

This collection is a long-awaited addition to the popular Toxic World post-apocalyptic science fiction series. It's sure to please fans and newcomers to the series alike.

Available in electronic edition!

The Scavenger (A Toxic World Novelette)

In a world shattered by war, pollution, and disease, a lone scavenger discovers a priceless relic from the Old Times.

The problem is, it's stuck in the middle of the worst wasteland he knows—a contaminated city inhabited by insane chem addicts and vengeful villagers. Only his wits, his gun, and an unlikely ally can get him out alive.

Set in the Toxic World series introduced in the novel *Radio Hope*, this 10,000-word story explores more of the dangers and personalities that make up a post-apocalyptic world that's all too possible.

Available in electronic edition!

The Last Hotel Room

He came to Tangier to die, but life isn't done with him yet.

Tom Miller has lost his job, his wife, and his dreams. Broke and alone, he ends up in a flophouse in Morocco, ready to end it all. But soon he finds himself tangled in a web of danger and duty as he's pulled into scamming tourists for a crooked cop while trying to help a Syrian refugee boy survive life on the streets. Can a lifelong loser do something good for a change?

A portion of my royalties will go to a charity for Syrian refugees.
Available in electronic and print editions!

The Night the Nazis Came to Dinner and Other Dark Tales

A spectral dinner party goes horribly wrong...

An immortal warrior hopes a final battle will set him free...

A big-game hunter preys on endangered species to supply an illicit restaurant...

A new technology soothes First World guilt...

Here are four dark tales that straddle the boundary between reality and speculation. You better hope they don't come true.
Available in electronic edition!

The Quintessence of Absence

Can a drug-addicted sorcerer sober up long enough to save a kidnapped girl and his own duchy?

In an alternate eighteenth-century Germany where magic is real and paganism never died, Lothar is in the bonds of nepenthe, a powerful drug that gives him ecstatic visions. It has also taken his job, his friends, and his self-respect. Now his old employer has rehired Lothar to find the man's daughter, who is in the grip of her own addiction to nepenthe.

As Lothar digs deeper into the girl's disappearance, he uncovers a plot that threatens the entire Duchy of Anhalt, and finds that the only way to stop it is to face his own weakness.

Available in electronic edition!

Writing Books by Sean McLachlan

Writing Secrets of the World's Most Prolific Authors

What does it take to write 100 books? What about 500? Or 1,000?

That may sound like an impossibly high number, but it isn't. Some of the world's most successful authors wrote hundreds of books over the course of highly lucrative careers. Isaac Asimov wrote more than 300 books. Enid Blyton wrote more than 800. Legendary Western writer Lauren Bosworth Paine wrote close to 1,000.

Some wrote even more.

This book examines the techniques and daily habits of more than a dozen of these remarkable writers to show how anyone with the right mindset can massively increase their word count without sacrificing quality. Learn the secrets of working on several projects simultaneously, of reducing the time needed for each book, and how to build the work ethic you need to become more prolific than you ever thought possible.

Available in electronic and print edition!

History Books by Sean McLachlan

Wild West History
Apache Warrior vs. US Cavalryman: 1846-86 (Osprey: 2016)
Tombstone—Wyatt Earp, the O.K. Corral, and the Vendetta Ride (Osprey: 2013)
The Last Ride of the James-Younger Gang (Osprey: 2012)
Civil War History
Ride Around Missouri: Shelby's Great Raid 1863 (Osprey: 2011)
American Civil War Guerrilla Tactics (Osprey: 2009)
Missouri History
Outlaw Tales of Missouri (Globe Pequot: 2009)
Missouri: An Illustrated History (Hippocrene: 2008)
It Happened in Missouri (Globe Pequot: 2007)
Medieval History
Medieval Handgonnes: The First Black Powder Infantry Weapons (Osprey: 2010)
Byzantium: An Illustrated History (Hippocrene: 2004)
African History
Armies of the Adowa Campaign 1896: The Italian Disaster in Ethiopia (Osprey: 2011)